WINTER

EMERGENCE

Dana Bell

WolfSinger Publications ⸘ Brackettville, Texas

DEDICATION

Dedicated to God because it was written with inspiration provided by him.

In memory of Dids, Little One, Tabitha, Sammy, Max, and Adara who await my arrival.

To my Cat Overlords Taj and Esther who fill my life with demands to be fed on their schedule, taking over my bed, insisting the door be open even when it's cold, using my flip flops as a pillow, and being jealous of the computer. They fill my life with joy, giggles, and love on their terms.

Author's Note

At a party I attended years ago, I met someone who had been inside one of the most famous military bases in the world. Many TV shows and movies have used the entrance as part of their setting. So when I got the chance to talk to someone who had been beyond the entrance, I grabbed the chance to gather facts for my story. I don't unfortunately remember the person's name, but I am forever grateful for their time and information.

Much of what is described inside the mountain is based on fact. Some came from my imagination and even folklore about a certain popular TV show during the late 1990s.

And yes, there is a well-known zoo close by.

Many of the places in this story are real. I destroyed them, covered them with snow/ice, and envisioned a frozen world. My characters live here near the base of the mountains.

Two things crept into the story. Moon, a feline of unknown origins, which will be revealed in the final book of the trilogy, *Winter Moon*. Shadow, a Chosen One who needed to be in this tale since she appeared in a story called *Doing My Job* and informed me what she had been assigned to protect. Her full tale is set in the far future and the distant past.

There are a few stories about the future after the ice age Word Warrior, his mates, kittens and others had to survive. There's even a story about the little girl mentioned in *Winter Awakening* and her fate. They are featured in a short story collection called *Bast's Chosen Ones and other cat adventures.*

Winter Awakening, Winter Emergence and the yet to be completed *Winter Moon* are set in the future. *God's Gift* is the prequel and shows all the plans set in place to save the human race covering a century of secretive plotting. *Pack Rule* gives the fate of their parents as told through the eyes of a wolf on the road to intelligence.

Homefall Search, set to be released in 2024, is the first book in a new series setting the stage for the arrival of the long-awaited Messengers. The next two books are already in the planning stages and have no titles yet.

The worlds of the Five Systems and Borders, including the characters, have been around for years. They've been waiting for their story to be told. The time has arrived.

These books are tied together in a multi-layered tale spanning centuries. Of course, the Chosen Ones insisted on being part of it and who am I tell them no?

PRELUDE

Mute thought long and hard about what he wanted to communicate and decided a simple message was best. The words appeared on the screen and he sat back proudly.

HELLO? IS ANYONE THERE?

Satisfied it was what he wanted to say, he hit Send. Now all he had to do was wait.

CHAPTER 1

KAT

Red splattered white met her eyes while the helicopter blade slowly churned overhead. Yips, ripping and screams filled her ears. A bitter tang stung her nose.

Horrified, she floated above the scene. Furred figures darted among the carnage. Her mouth opened, but her shriek never sounded…

Kat awoke screaming, her heart pounding so hard she felt as if it were going to explode. Vaguely it reminded her of the old movie they'd watched a few nights back. It had been filled with vile creatures that used humans to hatch their young.

She shook her head trying to push away both the horrific movie and her dream.

"Ned is out there somewhere. He has to be. He isn't…"

She couldn't finish the sentence.

A soft beep finally pierced her dazed mind. Kat glanced at the time and her heart sped up again. "By the mountain," she swore. "I'm gonna be late again."

Her feet hit the cold floor and she shivered. "I might just have enough time," she said as she hurried down the hall to the communal showers.

The hot water chased the last of her nightmare away. She toweled herself dry and tossed on the ugly green clothes almost everyone wore. Kat wasn't sure why. Some of their tradition's reasons had been lost through the centuries.

Rushing back to her bunk, she looked frantically for her boots. A brown toe peeked out from under the steel chair and she grabbed it, finding the other not far away. She also located her earpiece and plopped into her shirt pocket.

She glanced up at the mattress above hers. Empty. Kat suspected Lin, her older sister, had spent the night in hydroponics again. She'd been doing that constantly for the past six months.

Her stomach growled. She rushed to the dining hall to grab a banana, a piece of cheese and a cup of what passed for tea.

Munching on her food and sipping the lukewarm liquid, Kat trudged down the dull gray-green halls.

Taking a sharp turn, she entered the com room. She plopped down in the hard chair, earning herself a glare from the technician she was late relieving.

"Overslept again," Olga accused.

"Sorry," she mumbled.

The woman shook her graying head. Being the oldest of the com techs Olga had little patience with the younger ones. "Better learn to get up on time."

"Why? It's not like anything happens."

"With the exploration teams out," Olga lectured her—again. "You never know when they might need help."

"My brother never sent a message," Kat retorted.

"We expected losses. He knew that." The older woman glowered at her. "So do you."

Olga picked up the blanket she constantly kept with her. Several times Kat had heard the woman complain about the cold. Kat didn't agree. Either it was because there might be a problem with the heating system, or simply because of Olga's age. Kat would bet on the latter.

"See you tomorrow."

"As always." Kat tilted her head back and stared at the oversized ceiling. She pulled her hair piece out her pocket, it was something her mother said had been passed down since before the ice age started, and pulled her long, straight black hair up into a bun. She stuck the long wooden pin into it and hoped it would stay out of her almond shaped eyes.

"Now, how do I entertain myself tonight?" she muttered.

At first, she tried her brother's frequency. All she picked up was static. Next she flipped through the others, trying to find out if anyone on the teams had tried to call in.

Nothing. Silence. Boring!

Kat got up and stretched her slender limbs. She'd turned twenty only a few days before her brother left on his mission. They'd taken the helicopter out to search for the first one, which had vanished months before. The base hadn't heard from either since.

"Wonder if you found them?" She'd gotten into the habit of talking to herself during the long night hours. What else was she going to do? She had the worst post in the mountain.

With a weary sigh, she turned her attention to one of the neighboring computer monitors. The old machines weren't used very much. Mostly people accessed them when something broke or they wanted to review the old news files.

Although recently, one of the scientists had been using them to try and contact other computers that might still be working somewhere on the planet. He'd had limited success. Or so he said.

"Feel sorry for anyone who might have been near any of them." From the rumors she'd heard, he'd pinged a couple in the distant city. There hadn't been any type of answer. She guessed all the people were either dead or had migrated to the warmer south long ago.

"Well, I have nothing else to do." She sat down in a slightly more comfortable chair and switched on the power. They'd all been taught as children how to use the computers and just about every other old machine as well. The more they knew, the more they could operate and keep the base running. Mostly.

The screen lit up and she went through the various commands until she reached the main program. At one time there had been a service called the Internet and from what she remembered, sometimes they could still use it. Depended on what server they reached and whether or not it ran on solar power instead of the dead power lines. Most of those had been brought down by snow and ice.

"Now what might I find tonight and not think about…" she stopped herself. The long hours alone allowed her mind to roam too much and remember how much she missed her brother Ned. He'd held their family together after their parents had died during a hunt. One of the polar bears had come upon the group while they'd been sleeping in their camp.

"I will *not* go there." Randomly she hit a button and saw the email option come up. Well, why not check it?

Kat didn't honestly expect there to be any messages. Not with there being so few people in the world, or so their leaders thought. Maybe their group had been the only survivors. Or maybe those in the south had dropped so far back into barbarism all knowledge of technology had been lost.

She opened email and stared in surprise. A message! Out of habit Kat looked around the room even though she knew no one else was there. She considered alerting one of the scientists. She tapped her fingers on the desk. Maybe this was her chance to make a major discovery—like the animals several of the teams had brought back.

Kat moved the curser and opened the file. The message was simple.

HELLO. IS ANYONE THERE?

"That's it? No, Hi, this is so and so and I'm in such and such?" It was sooo disappointing. Their first contact with someone from the outside world and the message didn't give her information!

She pulled her hands up to her face and rested her chin on her fingers. Did she dare answer without talking to someone in charge? It might be fun. Her own personal secret no one else knew about.

Before Kat changed her mind, her fingers flew across the keys.

HELLO YOURSELF.

She hit send and held her breath to see if there might be an immediate answer. 'Message waiting' appeared. She opened it.

WHERE ARE YOU?

FAR AWAY. She returned. ARE YOU WARM WHERE YOU ARE?

NOT REALLY. WE KEEP WARM BY CUDDLING TOGETHER IN WOOL.

Now that was strange. She tapped out her next message.

CUDDLING TOGETHER? DON'T YOU HAVE YOUR OWN BEDS?

NO.

Definitely odd. Everyone she knew had their own beds even when they shared quarters.

I LIVE UNDERGROUND. No harm telling whomever that. It wasn't like they'd be able to locate her position. MY PEOPLE HAVE FOR A VERY LONG TIME.

HOW LONG?

YEARS. Safe enough reply. I'VE NEVER BEEN OUTSIDE. HAVE YOU?

COLD. WET. SNOW EVERYWHERE. DO YOU KNOW WHEN IT WILL END?

NO.

At least the other didn't seem to know anymore about when the constant cold would end then she did. Every time she asked the older adults she was told, 'soon'.

WHERE ARE YOU? Kat wondered where the other might be.

DON'T KNOW. MUST GO.

The emails stopped. Disappointed, Kat waited to see if the person would come back. After thirty minutes or so and no more messages, she resigned herself to being bored for the rest of night and shut off the computer.

She sat back down before the com and waited for her dull shift to be over.

~ * ~

At least her relief arrived on time. Kat rose, stretched her cramped muscles from sitting still for so long, and hurriedly exited out of the com room. Other people trudged down the dimly lit hallways, some opening doors to their quarters, others turning down side corridors to various departments and a few heading towards the cafeteria.

Whiffs of pancakes and eggs tickled her nose. Kat decided not to retreat to her bunk. She followed the enticing aroma, grabbing a tray and filling her plate with eggs, pancakes, and some sort of meat. At the end of room stood the coffee and tea machines. Kat filled a large mug and chose a table in the far back corner.

Sipping her weak tea, she felt its faint jolt revive her, which would help keep her awake for the next several hours while she struggled through the various lessons their teachers expected their students to study. Not that knowing history or some of the other subjects would be very useful in her day-to-day life.

"Hi, Kat." Her sister Lin primly sat down on the other side of the metal table.

"Plants no longer thirsty?" Kat took another sip. She grimaced. What she wouldn't give for a nice hot cup of tea.

"I needed a break." Lin nibbled on some toast. "Did you hear from Ned?" Her sister's oval face flashed a not so hopeful look.

"Not a peep." She wasn't exactly lying. There hadn't been any noise on the coms.

"You think he's dead?"

"I don't know, Lin." Secretly, Kat hoped he still lived.

"If he was alive he would have come back already." Lin paused before she added quietly, "Maybe we should have a memorial service."

"And maybe we shouldn't!" Kat snapped back. "We have no idea what is out there. He might have had to walk."

"Ned went to the city, Kat." Lin sighed, pushing her short black hair behind her ear. "There's probably all kinds of danger we don't know about."

"They never reached anyone there so I doubt it." She felt a tug of guilt about her secret conversation the night before. Kat ignored it. "Besides, Doc Pat didn't see anything dangerous about the animals the other missions brought back."

Lin shivered and grabbed her mug, taking a huge gulp. "They aren't normal animals though. Have you been to the observation room and looked at them?"

"No. Been too busy trying to catch up on my lessons." Truth, she'd chosen not to keep caught up. Ms. Hoffman, the base teacher, was forcing her to or else she wouldn't get her certification and be able to bid for other shifts or positions.

"You just don't want to do them." Lin knew her too well. "You think we have no need for any of it."

"Let's not talk about it. We'll just end up arguing like always."

"Fine." Lin peeled her orange. "Want a slice?"

"Sure." She accepted the slice and nibbled on the tart yet sweet fruit. "How are these growing?"

"Okay. We're still not sure if the nutrients are right. I think they're supposed to be bigger."

"As long as we can eat them, does it really matter?"

Lin's serious chocolate brown eyes studied her. "If we don't," she stopped. "Never mind, it doesn't matter."

Kat couldn't help the snort. "You take everything so seriously, Lin."

"So should you."

"And why is that? We've been down here for a long time. We're fine."

"Not really." Her sister spoke so softly Kat wasn't sure she'd heard correctly. "I have to get back." Lin got up and left, still carrying her mug and half-finished orange.

Closing her eyes Kat muttered, "Ned, I sure wish you were here."

CHAPTER 2

MUTE

Even if he'd never heard them, it was still strange to Mute to have all the other cats gone, except for during the day when Word Warrior and others held classes. At night, he and Sasha slept in the library, while litter mates Neutron and Sapphire denned in a closet.

Mute padded to the door, twitching his tail. He saw Algier dart into one of the classrooms. The other male had never gotten over the fact Sasha had chosen him, the deaf cat, instead of a strong Tom. Yet, it had been Mute and Word Warrior who had battled Midnight to protect the females and kittens, even if in the end, Tomura and the females had chased the rival away.

Algier had not been part of the challenge, nor had he tried to help defend what had also been his home. Mute simply couldn't understand the other. Not that he really wanted to as long as the other male stayed away from him, his mate and their kittens.

When the other didn't emerge from the classroom, Mute went back and jumped up on the counter. He sat before the computer, which glared white in the dark room. Once again he opened the email program and waited to see if there any messages. There weren't. Earlier, he'd contacted someone, but he'd had to stop when Sasha needed to go relieve herself.

He kept hoping he would soon learn his kittens' names. They were still too young to be left alone so he had to wait. They had two males and one female. He'd watched them being born and now, when necessary, he helped keep them warm.

Cocking his head to study the various functions, he decided he'd send out another message. Perhaps whomever he'd contacted would answer again. He raised his paw and typed yet another message and hit send.

There was no immediate response, which he found disappointing. He jumped down and nosed through another manual to discover more computer secrets.

He paused in his study when he sensed he was not alone. Slowly his head came up. In the doorway Algier stood, his gray striped tail violently jerking.

Mute took a step toward the other male, automatically puffing up his white fur to make him seem bigger. Something rubbed against his side and he hopped to the side, turning to face a new enemy.

Sasha stood beside him. Algier took a step inside. Suddenly she leapt and racked her claws over the other's nose. The intruding male darted back into the hall.

His mate came to him and gave him a friendly lick before returning to their nest to care for their kittens.

He wasn't insulted she'd intervened. The Right of Challenge, Sasha had told him, had already been changed by the females of this den. Algier probably had needed to be reminded.

Once again he took his place before the computer screen and waited for a response uncertain it would come.

Chapter 3

Nan and Jojo

"Jojo, hurry!" Nan bounced through the snow, her feet leaving prints any predator could follow.

The young wolf growled. He lifted his leg and peed against the odd metal structure marking his territory. His and Nan's.

She vanished around the corner of the busted blue and white building. Jojo trotted behind watching for any predators or smells of the wolf packs who no longer sent their pups to the school.

"Isn't it wonderful!" She stood under the partly hanging door. Her tan tail slowly moved back and forth, barely brushing the snow.

"Far from school." His instincts said they should have stayed with the pack. Being away made him uncomfortable.

"We can watch for the others." She turned her head to look at him. "See if anymore flying...helicopters come."

He remembered the death brought by the renegade packs. The two-legs had been killed after a cub's death. They all feared when the humans, if indeed that was what they had been, returned. There would no doubt be retribution.

"Come on," Nan urged. She vanished into the dark hallway.

Jojo cautiously followed. Dank mustiness met his nose and he sneezed. His back barely cleared the door and he decided they would have to find another way out. Otherwise, it would be easy for a predator or a territorial wolf, to trap them inside.

"I wonder what this used to be?" Nan's question floated back to him.

He hurried on long gangly legs to join her, his large feet leaving imprints on the wet dust and snow-covered floor. He joined the young cat standing in a huge room with walls a dingy orange. Along two walls odd gray structures lined them.

"I wonder what those are?" Nan asked.

"Not know."

"I guess we'll have time to find out." She padded back to him.

"Do we want to den here or above?"

Denning above was not a good choice, but it would allow them to do what they'd planned to accomplish. He pushed through the busted open door and trotted up the creaking wooden stairs. Although he couldn't hear her, he knew Nan followed.

On the next level the windows were busted out and most of the furniture covered in snow and ice. Hadn't been like that the first time they'd been here. He found the next set of stairs and climbed even higher.

"Oh, this is wonderful!" Nan bounded over and put her front paws on the low set windowsill. "You can see everything!"

Jojo joined her, having to admit the view gave them the advantage. However, he knew they could get trapped with only one way out. "Not sure."

"Why?" She didn't look at him.

"Could get trapped."

"Maybe." She slowly walked around the smallish room. He watched as she stopped beside a half broken out window. "We might be able to escape here."

He went to look over her shoulder. Nan had a point although it would be a very tight squeeze for him. If they were both careful, they might be able to jump to the slanted snow-covered roof, traverse it and slide down on the far side.

"Good find."

"I think so," she agreed. "There's more stairs."

"Explore later. Need to make warm."

"I know." Reluctantly Nan followed him back down the stairs and they explored the structure for anything they could drag upstairs to make their den warm and cozy.

In one of the destroyed gray things, they found a coat and Jojo dragged it out. After he pulled it upstairs and under a desk, he rejoined Nan who hunkered down, her tail jerking.

His sharp ears heard the skittering noises and he realized he was hungry. A small shape erupted from behind some broken timbers. Nan pounced, expertly snapping the neck.

"At least we won't go hungry," she shared.

CHAPTER 4

KAT

I should have skipped class. Instead I'm stuck here trying not to fall asleep. And Holz's voice just drones on and on. Where did he find this poem anyway? It's not like anyone actually remembers who wrote it.

Kat shifted in her hard seat and tried to at least pretend she was paying attention.

"Really concentrate on the images in this poem," Holz droned.

> "One claim still staked,
> rooted in the sandy ground.
> Proud lodge pole pine giant
> fallen, dead, decayed.
> Pale gray,"

Like some of the hallways, Kat silently groused.

> "branches busted, termite eaten,
> licked black on the edges by an old fire."

Fire at least I understand. Her finger followed the initials of a previous student. The letters R. M. scarred deep into the wood. *My parents told me there was fire in their grandparents' time. I wonder what would have happened if the base had been evacuated. Would I have even been born?*

> "No new life springing from its brown cones,
> no twigs of Osprey nests or fish bone remains,
> no legacy left of its ringed trunk history.
> Wind topped by the asphalt road,
> ignored by hungry bulging Elk,
> forgotten by the black bear searching for bees' lairs,
> overlooked by rushing Yellowstone tourists."

Like Yellowstone was ever real. I don't believe most of the old stories. And a place with scalding water shooting up in the air and boiling mud pots. Yeah. Right.

And just what is an Osprey anyway? Is a lodge pole pine like the ones I see outside? All green and spiky with snow pulling the branches to the ground.

Bees she knew about because they used them in hydroponics. The bees helped keep the plants pollinated and provided honey to sweeten the coffee and tea. The medics even used some for various illnesses.

"So," Holz continued, "who can tell me what images the poet used?"

Scrunching down in her seat, Kat hoped he ignored her.

"Terry?" Holz called on one of his favorites.

She sneaked a glance at the time. *Just a few more minutes. Then I can escape down to the pond and feed the ducks.*

~ * ~

Kat really wanted to know how those who had built the place, managed to get a lake inside a hollowed-out mountain. For that matter, how had they built the base to begin with?

A few drops landed on her head and she grimaced.

"Rain. At least I know what it is."

Years ago, she'd asked Ned how it could rain inside. He explained the snow overhead melted and trickled down through the gray granite, escaping through cracks.

Drip. Drip. Drip.

Very annoying.

Slowly she worked her way down the narrow rock path to the E shaped lake. Ducks quaked and the geese honked at her. They knew she always brought them treats.

Taking a seat on the worn wooden deck, she pulled off her boots and socks. Gingerly she immersed her feet into the frigid water. Something nibbled at her toes and she tossed some bread out. Several orange-red heads poked up and pulled the morsels under.

"Yeah, eat those instead of my toes."

The Koi were pretty, but large enough to be annoying. No one used the fish for food and she'd never gotten anyone to explain why. There were some trout as well and a couple of other species she didn't care to remember except when they ended up on her dinner plate.

"Here." She tossed more bread to the ducks and geese. They flapped their wings at each other as they fought over the treats. "I've got plenty." Kat smiled. This was the one place she could be pretty much alone.

"Except when we're having fish for dinner." Then Derrick, she blushed thinking about him, would come down with his buddies and they'd spend all day fishing.

Derrick had gone out in one of the snow cats along with the rest of his archeological team. They'd headed north to see what they could excavate.

"Wish 'em luck." Kat doubted they'd be able to find much under all the snow and ice.

A duck quaked at her and she tossed it a handful of bread. The creature took some in its yellow beak and poked its shining green head under water.

"Don't see how you can eat that way."

When she ran out of food, the ducks and geese floated away. She wiggled her toes and reluctantly pulled them out.

No one really kept track of what she was doing, but Kat knew she had some homework to do and then she needed to get some sleep.

Her boots on once again, she worked her way back up the path and re-entered the dull gray world she lived in.

~ * ~

HELLO ARE YOU THERE?

Kat excitedly answered the email. She'd been hoping against hope her mysterious new friend would email her again. She'd also hoped no one else would discover her secret.

I'M HERE. WHAT HAPPENED TO YOU LAST NIGHT?

Several minutes passed before she received a reply.

MY MATE NEEDED ME.

Mate? How old was the person? OH. WOULD SHE BE JEALOUS OF US TALKING?

NO. SHE CHOSE ME.

Women choosing their own mates? Now that was something she wished she could talk about with Derrick. Her cheeks felt hot and she glanced nervously around the empty room.

"Stop it. It's not like anyone can see you," she chastised herself.

IS THAT A GOOD THING? she asked.

IT IS DIFFERENT. MALES NORMALLY CHALLENGE FOR THEIR

FEMALES. WHOEVER WINS, IS THEIR MATE.

Sounded very primitive to her. Marriage choices weren't quite that bad in the mountain. Their leadership tended to put couples together who they deemed genetically compatible and would produce the best offspring.

Maybe the two systems weren't all that different.

SO YOU DIDN'T HAVE TO FIGHT FOR HER?

NO. SHE WAS TOLD SHE COULD CHOOSE HER OWN MATE.

BY WHOM? YOUR LEADER?

There was a long, long wait for the next message.

HE ISN'T EXACTLY OUR LEADER, BUT HE IS THE FIRST OF US TO LEARN TO READ. CAN YOU READ?

Reading a new skill? How far back had this group of people fallen? And if they'd just learned to read, how could they use a computer?

The more she talked with this person the more questions she had.

I'VE BEEN READING SINCE I WAS VERY YOUNG, she answered.

I TOO, LEARNED TO READ WHEN I WAS VERY YOUNG. WHAT IS YOUR NAME?

Nervously Kat bit her lip. Did she dare tell the other her name?

"Oh, why not. It's not like he knows where I am."

She typed. MY NAME IS KAT.

MINE IS MUTE.

Mute? What kind of name was that? Did it mean what she thought?

HOW'D YOU GET THAT NAME?

I PICKED IT. MUST GO. MY MATE NEEDS A BREAK.

"Bye," she said to the empty email box. Kat turned off the computer and stretched. In a few more hours her shift would be over. Her ears picked up the faint sound of air being pushed through the ventilation. Those who could, slept.

"'cept my sister, the doc and a few others."

Did Lin ever sleep? Kat wondered.

She returned to her hard chair in front of the com unit. Mechanically, Kat went through all the frequencies. No one ever called in. Why would be tonight be any different?

"Derrick Metcalf calling base. Come in base."

Kat almost fell off her chair. She grabbed the mic, pulling the ancient device over her head so she could answer. "Base here. Go ahead."

"We're caught in a very bad storm."

What was she supposed to do about it? "Understood. Procedure is to anchor the equipment and hunker down."

"I know that," Derrick snapped back.

"So what's your point?" she returned.

"It's the nature of the storm." He sounded puzzled. "I keep seeing flashes and hearing a rumbling sound."

"I have no idea what it is." Kat couldn't remember any of the hunting parties talking about such a storm.

"Me either. I'm making notes about it to bring back for study." *And you're bothering me why?* "Copy, that."

"Good to hear your voice, Kat." Did she catch just a bit of smile in his tone? "I waited to call until tonight."

"I thought you just didn't like Olga," she joked back.

"She is a bit of a grouch," he agreed. "Don't tell her I said that."

"Wouldn't dream of it."

"Didn't figure you would."

Static hissed over the line. "Derrick?"

"Still here," he answered. "We should be back in a few days. You wouldn't believe what we've found."

"Looking forward to seeing your discoveries." *And you,* she added silently.

"I'll make sure you get to."

She understood what that meant. Not everyone got to see what the teams brought back. Many in the mountain weren't even aware how many teams had ventured out. The only reason Kat knew was because of her post.

"Thanks. Take care and come home safe."

"Roger that." The signal stopped.

"You'd better Derrick Metcalf or I'll know the reason why." *Just like I intend to find out what happened to Ned.*

CHAPTER 5

INDRANI

Bright flashes, followed by shuddering thunder shook the tall building. Indrani paced the ancient, carpeted hallways, checking first to make certain the two cubs, Jyotis and Valmiki were not upset by the storm. She found them in one of the rooms, curled up on a mattress sleeping.

The young male's long tail flicked and he opened one yellow eye to stare at her. He closed it and she assumed he understood there was no danger.

The storm released another thundering boom. Her ears caught the cracking of wood and felt the entire building shake. Indrani snarled certain the snow and ice had collapsed some part of their shelter.

"What happened?" Jyotis sprung into the hall.

Her brother's head raised although he hadn't moved. His ears leaned in the direction of the noise.

"Part of the building collapsed," Indrani explained. "I don't think we're in any danger."

"You hope," the young female said.

Valmiki stretched his long body, his white and black spotted coat showing his developing muscles. "Maybe we should go see?"

"It's too dangerous."

"But you said we weren't in any." He blinked his eyes.

"That is why we'll stay here." Indrani shifted from one paw to the other. Her entire life had been spent living in mountain caves. Human dwellings made her uneasy.

"I like this." Valmiki jumping down and padded down the hallway. He brushed his muzzle against a stone wall.

Indrani and Jyotis followed.

The room he stopped in had a high ceiling and an odd stone wall reaching up to the ceiling. A tattered carpet spread out over the tile floor. Broken wood spread over the area. Indrani wondered what the purpose the place had served.

"You can see outside!" Valmiki bounded over and stared out the clear glass. Shredded cloth hung down over his head. His ears twitched as a few strands brushed them.

Indrani joined the cub. In the distance she could see the broken part of the building. As she had guessed, heavy snow and ice weighed down the structure. Busted wood stuck up at dangerous angles and shards of glass glittered under another bright flash.

"You're sure we're safe here?" Jyotis asked. She licked a spot on her shoulder.

"As I can be," Indrani tried to reassure the cub.

"Indrani," Valmiki sat, wrapping his long tail over his massive paws. He would be a respectably sized male when he grew up. "How did you come to speak the howler—wolf," he stumbled over the unfamiliar word, "tongue."

The old healer went to sit before the stone wall. Her yellow-gold eyes registered the dark smudge before the odd shaped opening. Inside, it was black and held an ancient smell of a danger she knew well. She'd seen the hot burning orange-blue destroy forests and kill any creature unfortunate enough to be caught in its deadly fury.

"Yes, tell us," Jyotis pleaded. She laid down, her front paws tucked under her body. Her brother joined her, giving his sister a friendly lick along her muzzle.

"It is a long tale."

Thunder crashed. Something jingled overhead and swayed. Indrani hoped it wouldn't fall.

"It happened thus…"

Mournful howls woke her from her hunting dream. Indrani raised her head from her white, black spotted paws. Her ears twitched forward as the howls echoed again down the deep ravine and into her snug, warm den. With them mixed the triumphant roar of one of the striped ones. The vibrating yowl made her stay still as if she were the intended prey and not the unfortunate howler.

As the dim light crept further inside, the howling grew louder. Perhaps a pack had lost one of their dominants. She'd watched from many vantage points during her hunts as the howlers had passed below her perch. They tended to follow a single pair and when they didn't, swift punishment followed in nips or sometimes a howler was forced to the ground, their neck locked in the dominant's powerful jaws.

Her tail long tail flicked back and forth as she listened. She rose from her pine scented ledge and leapt down to the smooth stone below. There she allowed herself a leisurely stretch, her long back arching out and pushing the last of sleep from her.

The howling continued. Curious, but not enough to endanger her life, even her people fell as rightful prey to the striped ones, she paused to wash a spot on her shoulder before padding to the entrance. Snow fell heavily, the land below her den covered in thick white. Indrani knew she would be difficult to see, although if a swiper prowled, she would be in danger if she dared to venture out.

She wondered why the pack hunted. In such a storm they normally denned or else burrowed beneath the snow like the large foot she liked to eat. Perhaps the striped one had found them and thought them an easy meal. Even a pack would have a difficult time bringing down the large, clawed hunter.

Indrani flicked her tail tip. The pain filled howls haunted her. As one of the rare healers her desire to help urged her out into the storm. Her survival instincts said to stay and avoid becoming the hunted. The striped ones did not forget when their rightful prey was taken from them. They were known, or she understood, to stalk any who dared to steal their meat and killed the scavenger. Rarely did any try unless they wished death.

"Arrr, arrr, arrr." The sound of pain as the prey was ripped to shreds made Indrani shudder. Normally even the striped ones broke the neck or strangled their prey as did she or the howlers. She'd heard other hunters who claimed these high places did as well. She had not seen them; but had smelled their urine marks upon the bark or sometimes an exposed rock.

Silence fell as the yips and howling stopped. The only sound she heard was the wind as the trees answered its hard clawed tear.

The hunt now over and the rightful prey eaten, Indrani could do nothing. She returned to her pine bough bed and lay down. She washed properly and prepared to sleep until the dark came. Hunger clawed her belly as she closed her eyes.

~ * ~

"What's a striped one?" Jyotis asked, interrupting Indrani's story.

"A great hunter like us, often white with black stripes. Sometimes they are orange with the same markings." Indrani paused.

"Your mother did not tell you of them?"

"She died before she could."

"Then I must tell you of them as she would have." Indrani had many cubs of her own. She knew what they needed to know. During the next few sunrises, she would train the cubs to survive.

"So," Valmiki swiped at his sister. She growled at him. "Did you hunt?"

"I did," Indrani answered.

~ * ~

With a leap she bounded out traversing the snow with ease. Her people had come to these mountains long ago from the high crags of another land. Not directly, but the memory remained. She was one of the few who remembered and sometimes shared the stories when others came to be healed.

She stopped on a small rise, listening for the howlers, striped ones or a swiper. Sound could be deceptive as it bounced off the black rock and traveled down the mountain. More than once she had to pause and listen carefully before choosing a path through the new soft snow. At least the storm had ended. A partial moon helped light her way.

When she reached a good vantage point, she used her sharp claws and climbed up into a tree. The branch swayed slightly under her weight. Hiding in its needles she watched the water place below often a good place to find easy prey.

A large foot hopped across, pausing to push its nose under the white seeking some sort of food. Not finding anything it kept going until it disappeared into the thick trees. Indrani wasn't interested despite her hunger. She wanted a horned one.

Another storm approached. She could taste its scent. Indrani hoped the fierce goddess Sekhmet would favor her. Her prey's meat would last for several days and she would not have to hunt.

Another shape limped to the water. Even from her perch she could smell the bitter stink of blood. A muzzle lifted as if checking for predators before its tongue licked the liquid. Indrani knew it to be a howler. Perhaps it had been injured in the battle she'd heard with the striped one.

The howler staggered a few body lengths before falling. She watched as its paws and legs shook. When it moved no more she descended out of the tree. No prey would come to the water place. Not with the smell of a rightful hunter. Seemed Sekhmet had decided Indrani should go hungry.

Surrendering to the goddess' decision, Indrani padded to the water. Her tongue lapped the cold liquid. She tried to ignore the dead howler. The creature posed no danger to her. However, others would soon come to ravage the dead.

She lifted her head and listened. Pine branches hissed at her. She also heard a faint yip. Looking at the dead howler she could see the distended tits. A female. Was there a cub?

Indrani dared to follow the sound while watching for other howlers who might be protecting their young. She also had to be wary of striped ones who also liked to hunt during the dark. A possible defenseless cub would be easy meat. Even for her.

The tiny yip led her to a hollow log. Carefully she sniffed about checking for protectors. She found no scents other than the female and what she suspected was the cub. Sticking her head in, she found the howler huddling against others and even she could smell death. There had been three. Only one lived.

Indrani dared to lower her mouth and lift the white cub out as she would any of those she had birthed and raised. Backing out she flinched as a biting wind twirled through blinding her temporarily. She waited until it cleared before trotting over the snow back to her warm, dry den. She could only hope the shivering cub would survive until then.

~ * ~

"Like the howlers who brought Snow Fur." Jyotis' tail whipped back and forth with excitement.

"He calls himself Mute," her brother corrected.

"I know he does."

They snarled and growled at each other.

Indrani lifted a paw and pulled at her claws. She waited until the two quieted before speaking again.

~ * ~

A few sunrises came and went. She'd placed the howler cub on her pine bough ledge. After she'd cleaned it up, of course. Its fur reeked of its litter mates' death. A stench she would not abide near her unless it were rightful prey.

Briefly she'd considered killing it for its meat. However, the fierce goddess had another side, one that healed. Indrani too had embraced this as her calling, despite the howler cub having no wounds. Still, no reason to deliver death to one so young. Not when she could possibly help it.

Indrani doubted the cub would survive though. She'd kept it warm with her own body, like she'd had when she'd last had cubs herself. Though its scent was not theirs, it needed her care. A muzzle nuzzled against her more than once and she hoped it did not still need milk. She had none to give it.

With a new sunrise it opened its eyes again and whined. She licked the cub trying to change its scent. Cleaning it didn't help much. Her tongue made it more tolerable.

"Stay," she told the cub. Her order was answered with tail wag and its tongue licked around her mouth.

Indrani jumped down, stretched and left her den. She relieved herself in her normal spot behind a thick clump of trees keeping her territory marked. On her return trip she startled a large foot. The hunt ended swiftly and she almost forgot to leave a blood offering for Sekhmet. She wanted to devour the large foot to appease her hungry. Barely controlling herself she carried her intended meal back toward her den to share with the cub.

Movement caught her eye. She stopped and stared down the steep ravine. A lone howler stood there almost invisible with its white coat. They too could be stealthy hunters and she wondered why it had allowed itself to be seen.

Nervous she had been discovered and possibly her den as well, she dropped her meal and stood protectively over it. She growled a warning. The howler ignored her and began to climb. The other stopped several body lengths away and barked, almost, if her ears heard correctly, like it was asking a question.

"What do you want?" she snarled.

Several barks and a yip. The howler advanced half a body length and stopped. Its tail wagged tentatively in what Indrani assumed a friendly gesture. Perhaps it was since she'd seen the cub do the same thing.

However, she'd seen such tactics when they hunted. She growled again.

The other dropped to its belly and lowered its head into the snow. Now that, she hadn't seen anywhere but inside the pack, as if she Indrani were a dominant and the other acknowledged her as such. When she didn't growl another warning the howler got up and slowly approached while still keeping its head low.

Since she did not see the rest of the pack and sensed no danger of attack, she picked up her prey and cautiously backed into her den. The howler followed slowly, glancing from side to side as if expecting Indrani to pounce.

Once inside she retreated near her water spot, a small round hole in the stone providing fresh water which never froze. There she dropped the large foot. The howler crept inside, but made no threatening move. Voicing another yip it again seemed as if the howler asked a question.

A whine came from her sleeping ledge. The other's blue eyes darted upward then swung its gaze back to Indrani.

"Yes, I have a howler cub." Not sure of the relationship between the two she continued, "Stay there. I'll get it." She leapt up, taking the cub in her mouth and brought it down. She placed the cub on the stone ground and moved away, giving the pair plenty of space.

The howler sniffed the body. Again two eyes looked up at her as the cub licked around the others mouth. Backing up the other made a noise in the back of its throat and vile smelling meat landed on the stone. The cub nibbled at it and ate its fill. When it was full, it sprawled on the stone, closed its eyes and slept. The other stood protectively close.

"I won't hurt the cub." *I don't like the way you feed your young. It's revolting. Still, at least the cub has eaten.* She'd worried about it starving since it had eaten nothing for several sunrises.

Despite the stench, Indrani dared to eat her large foot. She ate most of it deciding to save a few bites. She gathered them into her mouth and approached the howler. The other watched her. Dropping the meat she backed away. The other hesitated before gulping down the offering and then cleaned up what had been thrown up.

"I have no reason to harm you," Indrani told the other "The cub is strong and will survive."

"Cub," the other repeated.

Startled Indrani blinked her yellow eyes. Had the other just spoken to her?

"Cub," she acknowledged.

"Cub." The other nosed the small sleeping body.

The howler released a series of barks and yips. Indrani wished she understood. But, from what she'd just come to understand, the howlers too, were intelligent. Perhaps, they could learn to communicate, perhaps not. She could only wait through the moons to discover if they could come to an understanding or if they would continue to hunt each other.

~ * ~

"So that's why you understood Dermot when he came to you!" Valmiki jumped up, nearly knocking over his sister.

She hissed at him and swatted his shoulder. He pounced on her and the two rolled over each other a few times before getting stopped by one of the light-colored walls.

"It was the beginning." Indrani scratched her ear with her hind paw.

"How did it end?" Jyotis freed herself from her brother and came to sit beside Indrani.

~ * ~

The older howler stayed and through observation Indrani learned it was a female. Through the storms and sunrises the two learned to talk to each other. Not well, but enough.

The female's name was Aina and the cub was Culain. The pack had many fights with the striped one. They'd known they'd lost their dominant female Wynne and thought they'd lost all three cubs since the other had denned in an unknown new place.

However, Aina, the least one, had not given up. She'd left the pack and gone back to the water. "Found Wynne's bones. Your scent. Followed. Found dead cubs. You. Hard to track. Took many sunrises."

No doubt the storm had helped lose her scent. Still, Aina had found her.

"Help Culain. Good. Tell others," Aina stood at the entrance the cub playfully trying to tug at the female's ear.

Indrani had no idea if that would be good or bad. "I'm a healer."

Aina sneezed. "Not know."

"Means I help others who are hurt."

"Pack leave hurt behind."

She hadn't known that about the howlers. Perhaps given enough moons, they'd trust her enough to come. "Your pack can come. I will help you."

Aina gazed long at her as if digesting her words. "Pack grateful help cub." The howler female dared to lick Indrani's muzzle. "Friend to us."

"Friend," she agreed. Did she really want to be friend to a howler pack?

Aina bounded out with the cub running to catch up. Indrani watched them as they went down the incline to the trees below. She noticed the rest of the pack waiting. They gathered around the pair, yipping and leaping. The pack turned as one, howling their thanks, which she now understood, and ran together out of her sight.

Sekhmet, will I see them again? Indrani asked, not really expecting an answer.

It is a new beginning, the goddess answered.

To what?

The goddess did not deign to reply. Indrani hoped to understand, but as for this sunrise, she wanted to hunt. Another storm gathered, she could taste its scent, and she hoped Sekhmet would help her bring down a horned one. The goddess had already favored her.

Although, whether good or bad, she gazed where the pack had been hoping they did not return and kill her as was their way, only Sekhmet knew.

~ * ~

"It was a good thing," Jyotis told Indrani.

"As we have seen yes." Indrani looked outside. The thunder snow increased and she could no longer see the collapsed building. "We should rest now."

The two cubs curled together, their earlier quarrel forgotten. They bathed each other and fell asleep, their heads resting on each other's necks.

"Sleep well." Indrani settled down near them. Her tongue cleaned her fur and she closed her eyes. Outside the wind howled reminding her of the packs in the mountains.

As she drifted into sleep, barely, she thought she heard the high-pitched growl of a striped one.

CHAPTER 6

DERRICK

"Damned wind," Derrick muttered as he struggled to close the snow cat's door. The heavy metal fought his hands, but he dared not take off his gloves. If he released his hold the door might snap and fly away. If it did, then they'd all freeze to death.

"Wish the tents had stayed staked," Robert said from the driver's seat. He shivered as Derrick finally managed to get the door shut.

"Yeah, me too. Would have been more comfortable." His eyes could barely see the other tractor, containing the other two members of their team, Savia and Mark.

Glancing back in the cab, Derrick knew there was nothing there they could throw out into the storm. They'd need all their supplies plus the sleeping bags they'd managed to salvage after the fierce wind had shredded the tents.

"I can't imagine anyone surviving out there." Robert pointed out the squat window.

"Probably why most, if they could, fled to the south." Derrick couldn't imagine anyone actually wanting to stay and freeze to death.

"We still don't know if it happened sudden or gradually." Robert shifted and Derrick suspected the short seat was uncomfortable for the tall man's bulk.

"Unfortunately. The old news recordings give a few hints, but after losing most of them to that fire a few decades back," Derrick shook his head, "the loss of our history is tragic."

"Oh?" Robert cocked a thick brown eyebrow at him. "That why you studied and argued to become an archeologist."

Derrick shrugged. Didn't really matter did it? He'd won and here he was, on his first expedition and freezing along with the rest of his team. All because some of the earlier teams hadn't accurately described the weather conditions or maybe that's why they'd lost contact with them, a fact the mountain's leaders hadn't shared.

"Maybe." He pounded his hands together trying to warm them.

"Or maybe I just wanted to get out of the mountain and see for myself."

"Glory. It's all about the glory." Robert laughed.

Derrick enjoyed hearing the rich sound filling the cab. Made it not seem so hostile and deadly. He knew they could die out here and none from the mountain would come to find them.

"We have the right to know about our past." Derrick waved his arm. "Out there is a town. A town buried in ice and snow. We didn't even know it."

"Point taken," his companion agreed.

"Doesn't it make you wonder what else we might not know about?"

Robert frowned, his young face shadowing. "Careful, Friend."

"Yeah, I know." There'd been rumors floating around the mountain, quietly of course and when the whisperer felt sure the leaders weren't listening, about what happened to any who dared question. No one could confirm the rumors. Ned Waller for instance had and he'd vanished on his recon mission. Whether deliberate or by accident, Derrick didn't know.

"Although," Robert dropped his voice, "does make one wonder if that old scientist contacted someone and that someone isn't so friendly."

"Like our teams got ambushed?" The idea hadn't occurred to Derrick.

"Maybe." He heard a thunk and Robert rubbed the top of his head. The other had his hood up so Derrick doubted it had hurt. "These things need to be taller."

With a laugh Derrick agreed.

The snow cat rocked as a gust of wind hit it. Jagged white flashed followed by a horrible roar hurting Derrick's ears.

"Love to know why this storm is so bad," Derrick observed.

"No idea."

"I didn't think you did."

"I know." Robert winked. He had deep brown eyes and they danced under the furred hood.

"Too bad we don't have anyone who can." They'd lost a number of specialists in the long-ago fire. The disciplines they'd mastered right along with them.

"That fire cost us plenty."

"And then some."

Robert cast an odd look in his direction. "Careful."

"You going to tell our leaders?"

"I'm not stupid." Robert tried to stretch one of his long legs. He grimaced. Derrick had no doubt they hurt. "I don't want to go on a mission and vanish."

"No more than I do." Although the circumstances were suspicious, Derrick wondered if it had just been coincidence. Too much about this frozen wasteland they didn't know. Anything could have happened. Who would have thought their tents would have been destroyed by a snowstorm?

"Don't know of much that could down a copter," Robert went on.

"I think these winds might."

"Could be right. If they got caught in them, well," he switched legs, "then maybe we might have an explanation other than," he didn't finish. Robert didn't need to.

"Agreed." Derrick reached behind the seat and pulled out a thermos. "I think we still have some coffee from this morning. Want some?"

Robert nodded.

Carefully, Derrick poured out the still hot contents into tin cups and handed one to his friend. Robert sipped the beverage and smiled. "This is the way it should be served."

Derrick nodded. The lukewarm beverages they got in the cafeteria paled in comparison. If he had his way, he'd never go back.

"What are you thinking?" Robert asked.

His friend knew him too well. "Nothing realistic." Derrick sipped the bitter brew. Liquid rolled down his throat settling warmly in his stomach.

"Me, too." Robert lifted the mug and took a swig. "I like it out here."

"If we don't freeze to death. Do we dare turn on the engine to warm it up?"

Robert squinted at the panel's gauges and shook his head. "We ought to break out the sleeping bags."

Another bright flash zagged, hitting the snow just inches from the snow cat. Boom!

Derrick barely managed not to spill the last of his coffee. He shook his head trying to clear the ringing. "Robert?"

"I'm okay." The other shook his head. "Damn. That was close."

"What about Savia and Mark?" Derrick tried to see through the whirling snow.

"The talkies don't work, so we won't know until the storm clears."

"Damn," Derrick muttered. He was the team leader and responsible for all of them. He hoped the pair hadn't been injured.

"So," Robert finished his coffee. "What other rebellious things can we talk about?"

~ * ~

When Derrick woke hours later, night had fallen. Ice covered the glass and he knew it would take quite a while to clear it before they could move the snow cat.

Robert honked noisily. Derrick checked to make sure the other was okay. His friend had an odd snore and it concerned him.

Both of them had bundled up in the sleeping bags and wrapped anything else they could around their bodies. The warmer they kept their torsos, the less likely they'd freeze to death. He just hoped Savia and Mark had done the same.

The vehicle rocked again and seemed to shift a bit. Derrick tensed yet knew there was nothing really dangerous underneath them. The scan, brief as it had been, hadn't shown anything except solid ground below. Main reason he'd made camp here.

Not far away stood a towering rock base. On the top he had barely seen something black and thin. If time permitted, he wanted to climb up and see what it had been.

"Any more coffee?" Robert's voice broke the silence.

"Plenty of water. Better for us anyway."

"Wanted something hot."

"In the morning."

"You say so." Robert's irregular honk resumed.

Not sleepy and very cold, Derrick tried to shift the coverings to get warmer. He reached into the open glove box and pulled out the torch. Clicking it on, he pointed it out the window.

Doubt I'll really see anything. What the...?

He'd sworn he seen a flash of eyes.

He moved closer trying to figure out just what he'd seen.

Something large moved around outside. Derrick really couldn't tell what. The creature, if it had been one, blended into the falling snow before it vanished.

Turning off the torch he put it back where he'd found it. They didn't have any replacement batteries and they might just need it later.

Derrick tried to hunker down even further into the sleeping bag. Damn, it was cold.

~ * ~

Bright rays bounced off the distant mountain and bathed the cloud ridden sky in shades of brilliant pink and orange. Derrick tried to stretch. His arms had gotten entangled in the sleeping bag. He pulled them free and touched the cab roof.

"About time you woke up," Robert groused.

"You're charming in the morning."

"Same as you." His friend wiggled free and opened the door. "Going to see if I can get a fire going. I need coffee."

"Make enough for all of us."

"Will do." Robert went outside. Even more frigid cold invaded the cab before the door slammed shut.

Derrick shivered, slowly unwrapping himself. He needed to go. Reluctantly he went outside and found a private tree. Business done, he hurried over to his friend.

"Hard to believe we had such a horrible storm yesterday." Robert pointed at the cloudy sky. "Won't be clear today, but I'm guessing we won't get dumped on."

"Still cold." Derrick's breath came out in puffs of steam.

Robert thumped him on the back. "All part of the adventure."

"Coffee ready?"

"In a few." A little fire burned in a hurriedly made sizzling snow pit. Water trickled down as the white stuff melted.

With a frown, Derrick looked at the other snow cat. Frowning he sensed something wasn't right. "I'm going to check on Savia and Mark."

Robert nodded, his eyebrows knitted together. "Yeah, kind of wondered why they weren't up yet."

Derrick inched through the new layer of thick snow. He reached the other vehicle and found the door ripped off.

"Oh, God," he moaned.

Blood splattered the seats. Draped over the seat, part of an arm dripped. He backed away, wanting to throw up.

"They up?" Robert called.

Derrick shook his head and vomited what little was in his stomach.

"Derrick!"

Robert ran over to him. He heard his friend gasp as the other saw the gore.

"What happened?" Robert sounded like a lost child.

"I don't know." Derrick leaned back against the cab. His whole body shook.

"We'll have to report this." Robert's white face registered his shock.

"I know." Derrick tried to move and collapsed against the cold metal.

"You need some food." Robert tucked an arm under his friend and moved him away from the death scene.

"I…I can't eat."

"And your blood sugar is too low. I don't want you passing out and then me having to take you back to the mountain."

Ever practical Robert. He was right. Derrick just hoped he could keep something down.

CHAPTER 7

NAN AND JOJO

Nan lifted her head, her ears twitching. Light filtered into their den and rested on the invading snow around the broken window. She licked Jojo's muzzle. He opened one brown eye and closed it again, his tongue licking around his sharp teeth.

Rising, Nan stretched her bronze body, her hind legs extended as far as she could. She probably looked larger than she really was. She'd been the smallest of her mother's litter. She sat down daintily draping her thin tail over her paws. Her eyes blinked against the glare of the sun.

"At least the thunder snow is gone," she said. Jojo snorted, turning so he couldn't see her.

Deep new snow lay outside the window glittering like the stars did sometimes in the night sky. A cold wind whipped through and she shivered. She'd been warmer next to the wolf.

I think I'll go see if there's a mouse or a rat. Nan padded down the stairs, the walls protecting her from some of the chill. They'd been brightly colored once. These reminded her of the sun's rays over the mountains, except these had cracked and tuffs of white showed through.

Once more in the huge bottom room, she scouted among the odd gray things. Nan heard no betraying squeaks or scuttling sounds. Maybe her prey slept. She should be too. The thunder snow was the worst she'd ever experienced. The shaking building and loud noise had kept both her and Jojo awake. They'd huddled together, both shivering as the storm raged overhead.

"Were you angry?" she asked The Provider. She'd read in the odd book they'd found about past things. Great floods. Entire races killed off. The two humans thrown out of a beautiful garden.

Although what had unleashed The Provider's fury the night before, if indeed that were true, was a complete mystery to Nan. She could think of no reason for such anger. None of the cats or wolves had done anything to warrant it.

Or at least, not recently. She had not forgotten past events nor the reason she and Jojo now denned there. Word Warrior suspected the two-legs would return. All who lived near and in the school were in danger. The cats. The Wolfs. The Spotted Ghosts.

She shivered from a cold not born in the room. The Provider held all their futures. Nan had known the truth when all their pack leaders had last met. Lavena, Herne and Dermot had proved the most worried. They had the most unforgiving past experience with the humans.

Callie, their Elder, had told her stories, well, to all the kittens actually, about the past and the human glory days, if one could call them that. They'd been cruel to their world and to all the other creatures who had lived there.

Still, the question remained about what had happened to the humans and what truly had caused the long winter. Callie hadn't known. She didn't know when it would end either.

Her paws grew cold. Nan reluctantly abandoned her hunt and returned to her mate. Jojo sensed her, giving her a quiet welcoming yip. She nestled next to his long warm fur, his hot breath chasing away the cold.

CHAPTER 8

KAT

"Wyoming is thought to be north of us," her teacher, Ms. Hoffman shared. She pointed to tattered map hanging on the wall. Kat could barely make out the vague outline of the United States separated into smaller sections. Not like it really mattered anyway. "There is a great deal of confusion over what really happened."

Kat shifted in her chair wanting to be released so she could go get some sleep. The more classes she took, the more useless information she obtained.

"We do know many people escaped in ships."

"How is that possible?" Bill asked. He was a year older than Kat. "The water's all frozen."

"It wasn't then."

"How do we know?"

Ms. Hoffman took a deep breath. Kat knew the older woman's impatient signals. "Because there were rivers and oceans, that's why."

The entire class groaned. How many times had they heard those same words said? Or a similar variation when the questions they asked seemed stupid to their teachers.

"We do know," Ms. Hoffman went on as if she hadn't heard her class. "That Wyoming now seems higher in elevations than it originally was."

"And we know that how?" Bill inquired again.

Kat glanced around. Everyone watched and listened. Bill was in rare form today.

"Because we know."

"You know," Bill straightened in his chair, staring accusingly at Ms. Hoffman. "There seems to be an awful lot we're supposed to just believe. You don't really have any proof."

Ms. Hoffman put her hands on her hips. Like the rest of the adults, she was slender, almost too skinny. Kat could tell because the teacher's green clothes hung on her. Her brown hair she'd pulled up in a ponytail and the beginnings of lines were around her matching eyes.

"I know because the teacher before me taught me." Their teacher tapped her foot impatiently. "Unfortunately, anything else I could show you was destroyed in the fire many years ago. You all *know* that."

The fire had become an excuse for tons of things. Kat wondered how much longer they were expected to accept the same story.

Glancing at the clock, Ms. Hoffman waved her arm in dismissal. "I believe your English prof is waiting for you."

Kat inwardly groaned. Another hour before she could get to bed. She was so tired. After she'd lost contact with Derrick she'd worried all night, constantly trying to tune in his frequency and find out if he was still alive. She'd still had no contact when she'd been relieved.

Her class shuffled out. They passed the next group going in. Three rooms were dedicated to school. Kat sort of recalled in her mother's day there'd been maybe six or seven.

"Odd," she mumbled under her breath as she took her desk in the next class.

Holz stood at the front, his literature book open in front of him. "Turn to page one hundred five."

Obediently she did and wanted to scream. He had picked out yet another poem which would mean nothing to her.

"Again, I have a poem from an unknown poet." Holz grinned. His clothes were baggy on him too. His almost bald head had a wisp of white hanging down into his wrinkled face. "Bill, would you read please."

Bill rolled his eyes. "Mental Monster perched on stripped purple, tan and red of Morrison Formation guarding treasured dinosaur fossils,"

Dinosaur fossils? What were those?

"fern imprints, giant brown tree fragments. Silent."

"Thank you," the prof interrupted. "Sammie, if you will."

Sammi, a couple years younger than Kat, was shy and hated reading in class. She felt sorry for her classmate.

"No longer drilling black gold," her quiet voice continued. Kat heard the quiver. "stealing from ages past placing power, greed, wealth in clinched fingers of oil companies,"

"Very nice. Kat, if you'd finish it." He waited for her to comply.

Great. She also heated reading out loud. "who, once, profited from pumping, pumping, pumping, like a steel heart. Still now. Wind, the only companion."

"Who can tell me what they think this means?"

Silence greeted his question.

~ * ~

Lying in her bunk, Kat tried to sleep. The loss of Derrick's signal bothered her still. How could a storm be very bad? Yes, the mission had checked in, but still, it sounded awful in the background.

Kat flopped on her side and pulled her rough blanket tighter around her body. Was it her imagination or was it actually colder in her room than it had been earlier?

"This is ridiculous!" She gave up trying to sleep and sat up. She could vaguely see her breath. "What is going on?"

Definitely colder. "Don't tell me the heat is broken." She wrapped her blanket over her shoulders and stepped outside into the hall. No one scurried about.

Dare she find someone and ask or not? And would they really answer if she did?

Kat shook her head and went back to bed. Since she wasn't expecting Lin back, she took her sister's blanket as well and wrapped up tightly in them, putting them partially over her head.

Eventually she got warm and her eyes dropped closed. Only to open them again when her sister shook her shoulder.

"Kat, Kat wake up."

"Go away." She peeked at the alarm. Not time for her to get up yet.

"Kat!"

"Go away," she griped again.

"Kat, wake up. Right now!" Her sister shook her again.

"What!" she grumped, slowly sitting up.

"You need to move to different quarters."

"Why?" Her eyes barely registered the frost on the walls.

"The heat is out in this section."

"How'd that happen?" Her fuzzy mind couldn't comprehend the words.

"We don't know. Come on." Lin helped her to her feet and led her out of their quarters.

Kat's foot slipped.

"Sorry. I didn't see the ice."

"Ice?" Kat rapidly shook her head. "Ice?"

A thin layer covered all along the floor.

"Come on." Lin managed to get her to hydroponics. She settled her sister on a cot in the small office. "You can sleep here. I'll wake you when it's time for your shift."

"'kay." Kat slipped back into sleep.

~ * ~

Shadowy figures skulked along the shelves, on the floor and hiding behind chairs. Kat tried to see them clearly yet they kept vanishing just as she thought she'd found them.

A lone howl pierced her ears and Kat sat up, looking wildly around until she remembered where she was.

"I was about to wake you," Lin said. She set down a tray on the dull gray metal desk. "I got you some dinner and tea."

"Thanks."

Lin hesitated. "I really have to get back to work. There are some clean clothes in the locker there," she pointed at the green door. "There's a small shower through that door."

"Nice." Kat had always used the communal ones. Getting to take a shower with no one else around would be a treat.

"Go ahead and eat while it's hot." Lin vanished through the clear door. A brief scent of green growing things touched Kat's nose. Part of her envied her sister getting to work with all those living plants.

Kat sat at the desk and ate her dinner of mashed potatoes, salad and whatever meat had been prepared. The tea was lukewarm as always. She wrinkled her nose, drinking it anyway.

A quick shower and clothes change did wonders for her. She reached her arms up to the ceiling and frowned at cracks she hadn't seen before.

She checked the small clock on the desk. She had five minutes to reach the com room.

"Great. I can't even be on time when my sister wakes me."

She grabbed her tea, stopping to refill it before dashing to her station. Olga glared at her as always and puttered out grumbling.

"Same to you," she answered.

Checking the frequencies, she couldn't reach any of the teams, not even Derrick's. She glanced at the log and noticed he hadn't called in all day. Wasn't like him at all.

Activating the mic she called, "Hey, Derrick, you out there?"

Static replied.

"Derrick, come on. You have to be alive."

Hissing filled the room. Kat bit her lip. She couldn't lose him too.

"Derrick, if you don't answer, I'm gonna come look for you."

Silence. No reply.

"You know how dangerous that would be."

Still no reply.

"Derrick?"

He had to be alive! He just had to be!

"Derrick, answer me!" she yelled. Kat got to her feet, her eyes begging for the com unit to produce an answer.

"Base to Derrick, come on back."

The silence wore on her. She swallowed hard, the fear clutching her chest the same way it had when Ned had vanished.

"Derrick?"

"Base," a reply whispered.

Kat sank into her chair, tears threatening to blind her. "Derrick?"

"Hey, there Kat. We're alive. Mostly."

"What do you mean mostly?"

"Savia and Mark were killed by an animal. We think. There wasn't enough evidence for us to know for certain which one."

"What about you and Robert?"

"We're fine. The storm last night… I've never seen anything so vicious."

"But you're okay?"

"For now. We're hunkered down in the snow cat for the night."

"What happened to your tents?"

"Shredded by the wind."

"Oh." Kat knew she'd have to report Savia's and Mark's deaths. Their leaders wouldn't be too happy about it.

"We'll be headed back to the mountain in a few days."

"You sure you're gonna be okay?"

"As I can be."

As I can be. She didn't like the sound of that. "Any idea what kind of animal killed Savia and Mark?" Kat shuddered. She'd hate to die like that.

"No. Storm last night covered all tracks."

"You be careful." Now she sounded like a worried mother.

"Will be." A rattling noise in the background alarmed her. "What's that?"

"Just the wind. Blows a lot."

"Glad I'm not out there then."

"Glad you aren't either. I gotta go, Kat."

She missed Derrick and couldn't wait until he came back. "Okay. I'll note you called in."

"Thanks. Made some interesting discoveries. Can't wait to tell our leaders."

If they'll listen. His unspoken words hovered in the air.

CHAPTER 9

MUTE

HELLO?

Mute glanced at the computer screen. Light pierced the dark and he hoped it would not disturb his mate. Sasha had fed their kittens, washed them, and then decided to sleep herself.

He glanced over at her warm nest. Nestled against her gray body their three young slept. One of them moved its tiny paw clawing at the air. Another shifted closer to their mother before they stilled.

His attention returned to the greeting.

HELLO. His message read. IS IT SNOWING WHERE YOU ARE?

I HAVE NO IDEA.

How could Kat not know? Mute glanced out the window. Flakes fell covering the ground even more. Some light from the moon tried to pierce the storm.

IT IS HERE. CAN'T YOU SEE OUTSIDE?

NO.

That was odd. How could another cat not see outside? They always needed to know. Whether it snowed or not could make a difference in where they hunted. Rats they had. But getting a rabbit or a goose, when one could be found, varied what they ate.

WHAT DO YOU EAT?

The answer took a long while.

WHATEVER THE HUNTERS BRING BACK OR WHAT WE CAN GROW.

Grow? Mute cocked his head to one side. His neck itched and he scratched it with his back paw. He'd have to read more books to understand what the other had shared.

MY MATE IS SLEEPING.

YOU'VE SAID MATE BEFORE.

YES. SHE'S GUARDING OUR YOUNG.

GUARDING? IS IT DANGEROUS WHERE YOU ARE?

WE HAVE MANY THREATS.

WE DO TOO. MY PARENTS DIED BECAUSE OF A POLAR BEAR

ATTACK.

He'd read about polar bears. They were large, had long white fur, sort of like his only different, and everyone, including the Spotted Ghosts, stayed away from them. Mute had lost his foster mother to one or so he assumed since she'd never come back.

I TOO LOST A MOTHER TO ONE.

I'M SORRY. TELL ME…ARE YOU IN THE CITY SOMEWHERE?

Did he dare answer? WE ARE IN A CITY?

IS MY BROTHER WITH YOU?

YOUR BROTHER?

HE WENT IN THE COPTER TO FIND THE ONE THAT HAD DISAPPEARED DURING A STORM. NED NEVER CAME BACK.

Mute blinked his blue eyes. He remembered a wolf cub had been rescued, but his name hadn't been Ned. However, there had been two-legs. Two-legs that killed a wolf cub and had been justly killed by the packs.

Was Kat a two leg? Mute hesitated debating on an answer. If he said too much he could endanger them all. It would also explain some of her answers and why they seemed both strange and familiar.

He wished he could talk with Word Warrior. The dominate male lived in one of the houses with his mates. He wouldn't be here until after the sun rose to teach the kittens.

I will do nothing to endanger us all. I want Sasha and our kittens to be safe.

NO, he answered truthfully. NED IS NOT WITH US.

I'D HOPED HE WAS. THAT WAY, I'D KNOW HE WAS SAFE.

Sasha raised her head and crawled out of her nest. Their kittens restlessly wiggled. They missed their mother's warmth.

I MUST GO. MY MATE NEEDS ME.

He turned off the program and went to keep his kittens warm. Sasha licked his muzzle before she trotted off down the hall. Mute didn't know if she needed to relieve herself or to hunt.

His kitten's tiny bodies were warm and he laid his head on his paws. He vaguely remembered his mother. She'd died when he was young. His foster mother, the Spotted Ghost, had taken good care of him. Again, he wondered if she had been killed by the polar bear.

Dermot the wolf had brought him and the Spotted Ghost cubs to the valley and to the cat who could read, Word Warrior.

For the first time Mute knew he had home. He had a mate. He had kittens. He would do what he had to in order to keep them safe.

CHAPTER 10
WORD WARRIOR

Snow drifted down from the gray sky and I lifted my nose to catch the snow tang. Behind me I heard several kittens scampering up and down the stairs. They'd made a game and chased each other endlessly.

Starlite jumped up on the windowsill. Her long silver tail swished against the peeling white wall. She blinked her blue eyes. "One will come."

"One what?" I tugged at a claw, loosening the excess and spat out a bit of nail.

Her head tilted to one side. "I am not sure. There's an image covering an image. I don't really understand it."

Wind whirled outside, carrying bits of snow into the two tall pine trees. They bent and shook. Some of the ice, along with green-brown needles, dropped to the ground.

"I do wish this cold would end." Starlite shook her head, the bell she wore tinkling.

Lara leaped up to join us. My black and white Maine Coon wife licked my muzzle and stared outside. "More snow." She flexed a claw. "I like it."

Like me, she had large paws, which made walking on the snow easy. My other wives were not so fortunate.

"I will be staying with Callie today," Starlite told me. "She did not eat the rat I caught for her and she just wants to sleep."

"Should I have Indrani come to see her?" I sensed my mate's concern.

"Not yet." Starlite dropped down and padded back up the stairs.

Tomura joined us. My Purebred mate I had won, licked a spot on her tan shoulder before speaking. "I do not think our Elder will live through the next full moon."

"She is old," Lara agreed.

And she would be missed. I blinked my turquoise eyes and hoped we could find another to take her place. Our young needed to have someone who could tell them of their past. What we knew and remembered of it anyway.

I glanced into the room filled with broken furniture and those odd small houses. Mizty, my lovely calico, swatted Clomper, her kitten. He'd tried to hide because he didn't want to go to school.

"Mom," he grumbled at Mitzy. "I have Algier today. I don't understand Science."

"You didn't understand Reading once," I reminded him. I had taught most of the kittens their first letters.

"He'll be fine," Lara said. "Clomper is really upset because he liked one of Sheba's kittens and Algier challenged him."

Algier was becoming more of a problem. Sasha had run him off more than once. I knew Mute could defend his mate. Still, if the older male hadn't been an expert in Science and brother to Starlite, I'd have made him leave long ago. I hadn't forgotten he hadn't help defend our den against Blackie, when the other male had challenged me.

"Time to go, my husband." Tomura waited for me. I still found it amazing the proud Siamese had chosen me over the dominate Purebred.

I climbed out of the window with my wives and seven of my kittens. Soon my young would be old enough to mate and move into houses they wanted for themselves.

"Do you think we should move into houses farther away?" Lara asked as she walked beside me down the show covered road. "There are many more than just this one near the school."

"That is for each cat to decide." So far, our group lived the furthest away. Most seemed to prefer to be close to the school. Still, I could understand Lara's concern. The rabbits were harder and harder to catch and I feared we might run out of food.

The wolves had no problems bringing down larger prey, but they didn't really share. Not like they used to. Too many cats lived in the same area.

"Rowena will have her pups soon," Tomura said.

Mitzy trotted up to join us. The kittens ran ahead playing a chase game. Her ears twitched and she stopped. "Do you hear them?"

I stopped. So did my two other wives.

In the distance I heard yipping. Not the sound the wolves made. Different pitches echoed through and around the houses.

"Butt sniffers!" Mitzy ran ahead to stop the kittens.

I looked around. Several houses were around us; any one of them would provide a good place for us to hide. "Get them inside!" I yowled to Mitzy.

Lara ran to help her and the two females led their young into the nearest dull gray house. Part of the roof had collapsed and a tree had crashed into the main front window. Tattered cloth flickered.

"Go!" I ordered Tomura. "Help keep the kittens safe!"

"You can't fight them alone!"

"Tomura, go!" I nipped at her. She hissed before dashing off to join the other females.

I stood in the road waiting. My ears told me the dogs weren't far away. I puffed up my fur and waited.

Through a gap between two busted houses they came. They saw me; their leader howling. I hissed in response not moving until I was certain they hadn't scented my wives or young.

They got close. Almost too close. I smelled their hot stinking breath.

I dashed past two canines almost losing a paw as one snapped at me. Not far away a narrow way opened between the house and a leaning fence. I knew I could reach it. I had to!

~ * ~

I dared to look behind me. One butt sniffer fought to get between the house and the fence. He whined in pain as he pulled back. I heard the others race around the house. No doubt they'd try and intercept me on the other side.

With a leap I managed to get to the top of the fence. I heard a crack and I pushed with my hind legs, securing a hold on the tilting roof. I scrambled across the icy ledge to the highest point. The sniffers reached where I had been, pushing their black noses across the broken wood.

One noticed me and barked wildly. The others joined him, some even trying to jump up. My heart beat wildly and I took several breaths, trying to calm myself.

From my high perch I tried to find a way down and escape. The spindly tree was too far to jump. Another tree had long ago fallen, its deadly spikes a sure way for me to be caught and make me easy prey for a sniffer. Even trying to get down on the opposite side would leave me nowhere to hide. The chase would continue.

Sharp barks drifted upward. Their dark eyes burned with hunger and several drooled. If one of them got too close to the other, they'd snap at the aggressor.

What was I to do?

My bushy tail swished side to side and I growled at them. Battle rage, as if I fought for a female, grew in me. I wanted to fight. To scratch. To tear. To feel their hot blood in my mouth.

Vaguely I heard howls. Not daring to take my eyes from danger, I hissed again, trying to keep their attention on me. They barked and growled.

The yelp of pain came almost as a surprise. I lost my footing sliding downward. Frantically I tried to stop myself before I became part of the battle below. My claws hooked on a bit of ruined roof. I stopped although my tail still twitched and I hissed again.

Lavena whirled in the snow, her jaws clamping on a large sniffer's neck. Red splattered everywhere. Bitter stench tainted the air. The rest of the pack followed her as they shredded and killed.

I don't know how long it lasted, but when they finished, not one sniffer lived.

I had to fight the rage and fear inside me. Slowly I skidded off the roof to the red snow below.

"Word Warrior," Lavena stepped over the carnage, blood dripping from her long muzzle. "You are unharmed?"

"They didn't hurt me." I lifted a paw and pulled at one of my claws. A bit of ice had stuck there. Doing so calmed me.

"We came when Tomura told us of the danger." She took another step toward me.

I had to fight the urge to run. Lavena presented no danger to me.

"Thank you." Another reason I was glad the wolves were our friends and allies. If they hadn't come, I doubted I would be alive.

Herne shook his prey one final time. He opened his massive jaws and dropped the dead sniffer. "We'll go with you back to the school."

Finally calm, I cautiously worked my way through the torn fur and bones. The pack surrounded me as if I needed protection. Lavena and Herne led the way. Behind us huge bloody paw prints were left in the pristine white.

We reached the gap in the fence leading to the school. My wives rushed up the slight incline, the pack parting for them. Tomura rubbed against me. Lara managed to lick my jaw. Mitzy thanked the wolves. Starlite sniffed at me, her fur glittering like the night stars. "I knew you would be unharmed," she said.

She must have known more than I had. I thought my time of death had arrived.

"I though you wanted to stay with Callie today."

"She told me to go when I sensed your danger."

Together we padded down to the old brick building. I noticed one side sagged more than it had before. The weight of the last snow must have weakened it. We'd seen many buildings collapse. I hoped the school didn't, at least not with us inside.

"Do you want Indrani?" Tomura asked.

"I'm not hurt."

"Lavena?"

The dominate female shook her brown and gray head. "None of us allowed the sniffers to bite us." Lavena dropped and rolled in the snow, cleaning some of the blood off her thick fur. Her pack did the same.

My wives and I continued into the building. Many kittens scampered out of our way and into their various classrooms.

"You don't have to teach today," Lara said. She blinked her copper eyes, lifting a paw and licking it.

"Better that I do." I knew my position of leadership, both with my females and the others who brought their young to be taught, had to show my strength.

Starlite spoke, "They'd understand."

"I'm fine." I wanted to snap at her.

"He is fine." Tomura came to my side, her thin tail high and proud. "On to your classrooms."

My other wives padded away although Starlite looked curiously at me and Tomura before she disappeared around the open doorway.

"We were only concerned." Tomura licked my muzzle.

At times I wondered about females. Though touched by their concern I thought it really unnecessary. As a male, it was my responsibility to protect them. I had done so.

Tomura left me to teach her class. I flicked my tail and entered my room. Yellow, brown, green, blue and several other shades of eyes all looked at me expectantly.

I sat down, draping my black striped tail over my large paws. The book was propped up by one of the busted desks.

"A," I began.

CHAPTER 11

KAT

Splat. Water dripped onto Kat's dark hair. Splat. Another drop tickled her nose. Splat.

"Grrrr," she growled. The internal rain was annoying. She noticed even the weathered gray dock was soaked.

"Quack, quack." One of the green headed ducks swam up to her demanding breadcrumbs.

"Here you go, you greedy thing." She tossed several onto the water. A flurry of ducks and geese fought over the morsels. Even the koi bobbed up taking their fair share. "Better the bread than my toes." She splashed once with her feet sending a wave across the interior lake.

"I still wonder how they managed to build it inside a mountain." She leaned back slightly, her hands resting on the damp dock. Overhead she heard chirping and the rustle of wings. The birds were a new addition. One of the teams had brought them back and they hadn't yet been able to identify them with the records they had left. Many speculated on how they'd survived the cold.

She watched the white wings tipped in black. One bird swooped down, skimmed the water and rose up to land on the large pole at the end of the dock. Opening its beak it uttered a piercing call and another joined it.

"Maybe I should go visit the other animals brought back." Kat got up, grabbed her boots and padded up the trail. At the top she slipped the heavy leather on her chilled feet and glanced both ways. She'd skipped classes today and didn't want to be seen.

No one seemed to be about so she hustled over to the rarely used stairwell. The door squeaked loudly and she cringed. Ducking inside she started down.

Originally there'd only been the surface buildings built on huge hinges. No one knew why. As the centuries progressed and because they needed more room, some industrious person or group had burrowed downward.

Not that many lived so far underground anymore. Over the last couple of centuries their numbers had been dropping. No doubt one of the many reasons their leaders now arranged matings.

Remembering that, Kat wrinkled her nose. She wouldn't have to participate for another year or so. Their leaders normally waited until the twenty first or twenty second birthday.

"And just my luck, I'll get stuck with one of the slimy old men." She shuddered. Her thoughts turned to Derrick and she wondered how it would feel to be with him. "Stop it!" she scolded herself. "Don't think such things."

The overhead light flickered. "Stupid, you should have brought a torch. "The lighting had a habit of failing at the wrong moment. She didn't know if the reason was because of the old system or the glitchy power plant.

Kat hurried down the last two flights and eased open the door. The dim hall lighting greeted her. She slid out and tip-toed along the stone flooring. None of the fancy tile or wood here just chiseled gray black rock.

Stopping at the correct entry, she puzzled over the writing on the old door. S something Command. Underneath it read Storage.

"No idea what that means," she mumbled before entering the room.

Around her tall red flowered vines draped an odd incomplete circle device. Tall yellow-green grass shivered at the slight wind her entrance caused. Overhead powerful lights mimicking sunlight illuminated and warmed the large rock walled room.

A brown head with long ears popped up, its pink nose twitching before the creature vanished back into the grass. Kat could see the movement, yet not the animals. No doubt she'd frightened them.

"Too bad they only brought the small ones here." Anything larger had been slaughtered and given to the cafeteria.

Except the wolves. They'd been given to one of the trainers hoping they could be tamed and used for various scouting missions. They'd had varied degrees of success or so said the rumors she'd overheard.

Kat edged her way along the wall and found a huge boulder to sit on. Staying quiet she hoped maybe some of the inhabitants would show themselves.

Minutes later, one of the creatures poked its head out and blinked yellow eyes at her. A sleek furred body with a long fluffy tail emerged, cautiously approaching Kat. After a couple steps forward, it jumped back, almost like she'd startled it. "I'm not going to hurt you," she said softly. In a way, it reminded her of the rare Mountain Lion her sister Lin spotted now and again. Only it was smaller and the fur longer. Not to mention the beautiful black and orange markings.

Slowly, Kat extended her hand. The creature extended its head as far as it could reach without getting closer and barely sniffed her fingers. "See. I'm not dangerous."

Evidently her visitor didn't think so either. Sitting down, its tail draped over its paws and cleaned a spot on its shoulder with a bright pink tongue.

"You're very pretty."

Again the eyes blinked at her. Ears flicked forward almost as if it were listening to her.

"You can hear me, can't you?"

The creature rose, stretched and vanished back into the grass.

"Bye to you, too." Kat sighed. So much for her sister's comment about the animals being different. She didn't see any behavior indicating otherwise. More likely just adaptions they made to survive. Just like they did too inside the mountain.

The light above dimmed a bit. "I think I'd better go." Kat left and hurried up the stairs. She hoped nothing went out since she had no desire to get stuck there until someone figured out she was missing and went looking for her.

Not that they wouldn't be looking for her anyway. Skipping class except to cover a shift was not ever acceptable. Kat knew she'd hear it from Lin later. Maybe. Definitely Ms. Hoffman next time she attended class.

Back on the main level, she checked the corridor and then hurried across back to her quarters. Once safely inside, she kicked off her boots and flopped down on her bunk, ignoring the cold. Her fingers found the secret book and she pulled it out from under her mattress.

The dull red cover with shades of sparkling blue, green and gold mixed in seemed to shiver in her hands. Kat had no idea what kind of creature slithered over the soft fabric. She opened the yellowed pages and started reading.

Granted, she'd read it many times. The words kept her connected to her family's past. She just kept it hidden from her sister since her brother had been entrusted with it first. He'd given it to her before he'd left and if, when he returned, she'd give it back to him.

Inside the mountain it is always so dark. The huge entry driveway was long ago covered with huge metal doors. The idea, I think, was to give us more room. Mostly, it is where we keep the crates and boxes of supplies.

Not to mention the various trucks and such. My brother Luke seems to think we might need them some day. Not any day soon if I'm any judge.

There are some odd rumors floating around about secret missions and sanctuaries the public wasn't told about. I know some of the military and their families evacuated to the south where it would be much warmer.

However, that's not what the recording Luke had heard said. He didn't really share the information with me. He was plenty mad though. More than I've ever seen him. He cursed the government and said we all deserved the chance and who were they to play God!

I might be upset too if I knew what he'd found.

"Too bad you never actually explained," Kat grumped. She turned to the next page.

There have been a couple of suicides. Luke said they'd taken some pills and died in their sleep. We knew there might be a danger of that. Both from what happened and so many lives disrupted and lost. Entire families have been wiped out. Not to mention animal species.

Almost surreal now. The huge billowing gray-black cloud. The lightening flashing and crackling through it. The intense heat as it swallowed the land.

I remember watching the skyscrapers rock and vanish. The cut off screams as people died. Luke and I were near a cave. We rushed inside after voicing our warning.

Some of the visitors there believed us. Others didn't.

I don't remember how long we were in that cold, damp place. We had very few supplies. We managed to supplement them with whatever we could find in the snack bar.

We emerged later to a world that looked like an alien planet. Gray everywhere. A sky rocking shades of red and orange I've never seen before or since.

Luke suggested we cover our mouths and noses. As it turned out, it was a good thing we did. Many in our group died who didn't follow our example.

Somewhere in town we met a National Guard unit. They transported survivors up to the mountain. Since there was little else we could do, we went.

I'm glad we did. At least we're alive.

"If you call this living." Kat closed the book and put it back into its hiding place.

She rolled over onto her back and stared at the underside of her sister's seldom slept in bunk. A few springs had broken.

Lacing her fingers she tucked them under her head. Kat didn't really understand what had happened. Some of the scratchy early records they had showed a huge cloud, but said nothing about the cause or even the consequences.

She knew they'd retreated to the mountain and until recently, hadn't really ventured out except to hunt. The cold and ice made the land uninhabitable.

"Did the cold kill you, Ned?" she asked her missing brother. "And what about you, Derrick? Will you safely make it back?"

~ * ~

Kat was bored. She stared at the silent com unit and glanced around the tomb-like empty room. Even the computer had been quiet. No secret messages from her unknown friend.

She did wonder though if she'd said something to upset Mute. Her mystery friend had been silent for several nights and no new messages had arrived. Or maybe he'd felt threatened by her inquiries about Ned.

"Or maybe you lied to me about Ned. Maybe he's your prisoner." She knew there was no guarantee other human groups, if there were any, would be friendly. She laughed at herself. Of course there had to be some. She'd talked to one.

Rising, Kat stretched her arms and wished she'd brought some popcorn from the cafeteria. The salty kernels would taste good right now. Instead she sipped her cold tea and grimaced.

Her relief would not show up for several more hours. What to do?

CHAPTER 12

DERRICK

Derrick was guessing the structure had been large. He dug out a corner of it, a large pile of snow witness to his efforts.

"I think they're brick," he said to Robert.

His friend grunted. "Too bad the roof collapsed. Maybe we'd get an idea on how tall it once was."

Pushing his fingers down to what he thought to be the ground, Derrick yelped as his fingers pushed through and he almost fell. He grabbed the edge sighing in relief. "This isn't the bottom."

"Really?" Robert looked up from his notepad. He'd been scribbling notes as they made their discoveries. "You think maybe we're standing where the roof once was?" His friend tried to look concerned, but Derrick didn't miss the twinkle in Robert's brown eyes.

"Might be." Derrick reached behind him and grabbed a pole they used to check the ground. He shoved it down the hole he'd found and broke loose some of the snow and ice, which fell below, smashing against what looked to be a hard floor. "Game to find out?"

"Why not?" Robert grabbed some rope, securing one end around the snow cat. He tied the other around his waist. "I'll go first."

"Hey, I made the discovery."

"Means nothing to me." Robert perched himself near the corner and wormed his way down the hole into the darkness. "Hey," he yelled up as he untied the rope. "Grab a couple of torches."

"Will do." Derrick ran back to the cab and rummaged around for the torches. One of them they'd taken from the destroyed snow cat. He stuffed them in his bulky pockets and hurried to join his friend. Once his boots hit the hard floor, he quickly loosed himself and grabbed one of the lights. He handed the other to Robert.

"We stick together," Robert said.

"Agreed." He shined the torch up. The feeble light barely touched the ice packed roof. "Think it will fall on us?"

"If it does," Robert shrugged, "we won't have much warning." He grinned. "And we'll be dead so we won't really care."

"Thanks a lot."

"Isn't like you have a girl waiting for you."

Derrick chuckled, but wondered if his friend's comment was true. He'd gotten the feeling Kat cared for him, although whether or not the leaders would put them together... He shook his head. No need to think about that right now. He'd made a new discovery and wanted to explore.

He flashed the torch around, frowning at the unfamiliar objects. Along one side there appeared to be giant metal doors. A couple of chains hung down and were covered in ice. All around them were pots, statues, and shriveled up trees.

"I wonder what this used to be?" Derrick was amazed. He couldn't see very far ahead yet the space seemed to be huge.

Robert took a few steps forward and Derrick followed. They wandered the huge maze. He saw hundreds of shelves and racks, most of which were empty. Derrick could only guess what they had once contained. Near one side, where he surmised from the broken glass on the floor, had been the entrance. Several odd desks with shredded rubber stood close by.

"Could this once have been a store?" Derrick wondered.

"Maybe." Robert rubbed his jaw. "I need to shave."

Derrick laughed. "We both do. We can clean up once we get back to the Mountain."

Near the back they found a wall of ice. They followed it around. Seemed obvious it had smashed whatever had been there. Derrick saw broken bits of wood and metal.

"Wouldn't have wanted to be in here when that happened," he said pointing at the damage.

"I'm betting," his friend replied, "most of the people were long gone by then."

"I sure hope so."

Following the ice wall, they worked their way back to the opening they'd found. Robert poked his torch into his pocket and climbed the rope back to the surface. Derrick did the same.

Back outside, Derrick took a deep breath of cold air. "Not looking forward to another night in the cat."

"Me either." Robert looked back at the ruins. "Maybe we could sleep down there. Might even be able to have a fire."

"Or the heat will melt the ice and bring it down on us." Derrick actually thought it unlikely, but he had to voice his worry.

"You and I both know we don't need to worry about it."

Derrick shrugged even as he went to get his sleeping bag and gear. "You never know."

~ * ~

The fire crackled inside the huge pot they'd used. Derrick had touched the side and yanked his hand away. His flesh burned.

Robert laughed at him. "Serves you right."

They drank hot coffee and finally settled down on the hard cold floor. Derrick propped his head up with his arms and stared at the flickers on the ice above. Strange shapes stretched and wiggled sort of reminding him of the few remaining old records they still had.

"Think we'll ever really know what happened?" he asked Robert.

"Do we need to?"

"Don't you want to know?"

He heard the other shift in his sleeping bag. "We're alive. I think that's all that matters."

"Yeah, but for how long? You know why the leaders are allowing us to explore."

"You'd best keep those thoughts to yourself."

"Won't take everyone else long to figure it out." Derrick had heard whispers. Others in the Mountain were beginning to suspect. The power outages, the failing crops, the continued machine failures they couldn't fix.

"Go to sleep," Robert groused.

Derrick heard the sound of zipper being closed and not long afterward heavy honking snores.

Moving his sleeping bag closer to the radiating rust colored pot, Derrick allowed the warmth to penetrate his body. He'd gotten so used to being cold the warmth was both an odd relief and an annoyance.

"So what are you up to tonight, Kat?" he asked quietly. He could almost see her at the com, staring at the ceiling, completely bored. She had the worst duty. Once or twice he'd snuck in to visit with her and had heard her talking to herself as she switched from frequency to frequency. Kat always worried about Ned and wanted to know what had happened to her brother.

He wanted to know as well. Derrick had hoped to encounter some of the other exploratory teams. He'd tried a few times, yet hadn't received any response. He knew for a fact none of them had returned to the Mountain.

Pops sounded from the pot. He jumped. Nothing to worry about Derrick reassured himself.

He zipped his bag up tight. The light from the fire actually keeping him awake. Turning so his back was to it, he closed his eyes, blocking out the brightness.

Slowly, the warmth penetrated his body and he dropped into an uneasy sleep. In his dreams huge snarling shadows chased him. He felt sharp rips in his flesh and he screamed.

"What the!" Robert yelled.

Shaking, Derrick woke up.

"What were you screaming for!" his friend demanded.

He brushed a hand over his face. "Bad dream."

"Must have been really bad for you to be screaming like that."

"Sorry. Didn't mean to wake you."

"Happens." There were rustling sounds. "Go back to sleep. And don't have any more bad dreams."

"I'll try." Derrick shivered, shifting so his front faced the warm pot. Why did he have the feeling the dream foreshadowed some future event?

CHAPTER 13
NAN AND JOJO

Cold trickled down her back. Nan snuggled closer to her mate. Even his body heat wasn't enough to keep her warm. She opened her eyes. Deep snow had invaded their high perch and coated the windows with ice. The wind blew tossing more white on top of them.

Nan stretched her lean body. She licked a spot on her shoulder and twitched her tail. More snow blasted inside.

"Jojo." She carefully placed a paw on his nose.

He sneezed and growled.

"I'm cold."

His brown eyes snapped open. "Lay next to me."

"I was and I'm still cold." She scratched in the growing snow. "I think we need to move."

Her mate lifted his head and gazed around. She knew the wolves would often bury themselves in the snow and still be warm. Nan couldn't do that.

"Go below." He got to his feet, shook his body, the wet white splattering everywhere. She hissed and backed away. Taking the coat in his jaws he followed her down the stairs.

They resettled in the orange room with the gray things staring at them like they were rightful prey. They didn't live, Nan understood that, but that's how it felt to her.

Jojo dragged the coat into the corner. The walls would guard their backs. He sank back down and put his massive head on this paws. His tail wagged brushing against the fading color.

Nan's nose detected many rats and her ears heard their scratchings. They'd be hunted later. She scampered over to Jojo and nestled against him, his thick fur warm and comforting.

Was it her imagination or did it seem colder than normal?

Thunder roared overhead, the gray things squeaking and rattling. Nan closed her eyes, rolling her body into a tight ball and tucking her tail over her nose. She heard Jojo breathing next to her and soon she drifted into an uneasy sleep.

The storm kept waking her up. Every time the thunder sounded it felt like the entire building shuddered and groaned. She heard Jojo snarl as he shifted restlessly.

There'd been many normal thunder snows. The recent ones had been more violent. Nan didn't know why nor did Algier despite what he understood about science. He had no explanation of why the storms had gotten worse.

A very loud roar sounded overhead. She sprang to her feet hissing. Jojo stood beside her, his teeth showing. He growled deep in his throat.

One of the gray things tumbled over. Crash! Several rats leapt out and ran out of the room. A blinding flash penetrated their den followed by another deafening rumble, causing the walls to shake.

A creature ran in. Long and sleek like the snow ghosts except instead of spots in had long black stripes. Also, it was much, much larger.

Nan wasn't sure why she sunk to the ground to make herself smaller. Jojo started to move forward. She nipped his paw. He yipped in surprise.

Two huge yellow-brown eyes turned in their direction. She saw the hind quarters bunch and knew they were about to be attacked.

"Run!" she yowled.

Crackling overhead and one of the walls sagged. A huge hole appeared and Nan jumped through it. She dared to glance behind her. Jojo pushed through the gap and floundered. A huge paw reached through and almost swiped his tail.

Breathing hard, she forced herself to stop. Jojo ran to join her. The huge feline attempted to pass through the same hole. The predator's bulk prevented passage and she saw its massive head disappear.

"Come after us."

"It'll have to go around." Nan glanced wildly around her. There had to be a place for them to hide!

"This way." Jojo dashed past the mesh fence. Not far away stood another building. Nan ran after him.

The window had broken long ago. Jojo leaped through it and skidded across the icy floor. Nan did the same. On the other side of the room were small toys resembling the human trucks she'd read about. Her mate found another open window and she followed him out.

Snow whipped around them making it almost impossible to see. She felt a mouth on her neck. Jojo's familiar scent told her she had nothing to fear. Allowing her body to go limp, her mate carried her across an expanse, around a large building, up some stairs and into another room.

He gently put her down, giving her a wet lick.

"Is it following?"

"Don't know."

A whirlwind of white kept the outside secret. Nan jumped up on a shelf so she could see. Jojo's front paws rested beside her.

Vaguely she saw the long feline shape saunter past. It didn't look in their direction. Instead, it lifted its great muzzle as if to taste the air. She heard its snarl and it spat snow.

"Storm mask scent." Jojo dropped down and began searching around the old store. He bumped something that rattled when it hit the floor.

"Do try to keep quiet." Nan hoped their intruder hadn't heard. Evidently it didn't since it continued trudging through the snow. When she could no longer see the invader, she jumped down to find out what Jojo was doing.

He stood behind a long counter. Her nose detected a hint of rat so Nan hoped they'd have something to eat. Jojo poked at something and one of the creatures squeaked. He closed his jaws around it. His jaw crunched it and rodent stopped struggling. Her mate put it on the floor. "Share."

"Good idea." She ate part of it. When she finished, Jojo gulped the rest down. Nan bathed herself and then looked around. "What now?" Word Warrior and the others should be warned about this new danger.

"Tired. Sleep." Jojo pulled some things that looked like creatures, yet didn't smell like them. He piled a few on the floor and made himself comfortable.

"The storm did keep us awake." She snuggled beside him.

A howling like the wolves sounded and Jojo lifted his head. A mournful noise escaped his mouth. In the far distance there seemed to be an answer.

"Not your pack." Nan was sure of that.

"One of the others." Far in the distance another wolf sang. "Not close." He moved his body so he protected her. His head faced the entrance despite the fact they'd hidden.

Warmth reached her body and Nan dared to close her eyes. When they woke they'd have to go find Word Warrior, after they dined on another rat. She didn't want to make the cold trek back to the school without something in her stomach.

Faint thunder sounded as the storm moved away. Nan was grateful.

She fell asleep listening to Jojo's heartbeat along with the feel of his warm fur.

CHAPTER 14

MUTE

Snow whirled outside blanketing the skeleton trees and covering the objects in the ancient play yard. Mute jumped down to the chilly floor, his tail jerking from side to side. He hadn't heard the storm as it passed overhead, but he'd felt it as the school shook. One of the outer buildings had collapsed completely. Luckily, it hadn't been the one where the wolf pack lived.

Padding down the corridor he returned to the library. Sasha curled tightly in her nest, his three kittens snuggled next to their mother almost lost in her fur. He jumped up on the counter and turned on the computer.

A message awaited him.

HAVEN'T HEARD FROM YOU FOR A LONG WHILE. YOU OKAY?

Mute hesitated. The danger they could all be in warred with his curiosity. If Kat was a two-leg, and he began to suspect she was, did he dare to keep talking with her? Still, he had a chance to learn more about their world beyond the school and not just what he remembered of their mountain journey to the city.

I AM FINE.

Glaring white answered him and no quick response. Mute decided to leave the computer on and jumped down, hissing when he saw Algier only a body length away from Sasha. He leapt on the intruder and the two tumbled across the cold floor and into the hallway.

He was vaguely aware of kittens scampering out of the classrooms. Algier wiggled free and bared his teeth. They circled, both with fur tuffed and their backs arched.

Where Word Warrior came from, Mute didn't see. The dominate male placed himself between them, his claws ready to strike.

Mute snarled and backed into the library. Algier made a step to follow. Word Warrior stood in front of the door until the intruding male angrily swished his tail and retreated.

Kittens hurried back into the various classrooms and Word Warrior entered one as well. Mute waited. Algier did not return.

When he calmed down, Mute jumped up on the counter. Sasha waited for him.

I WOULD NOT HAVE ALLOWED HIM TO HARM OUR KITTENS, she typed.

I KNOW, he answered.

I'M PROUD YOU DEFENDED ME. YOU'RE A GOOD MATE.

Her words made his sides vibrate. He brushed against her and she licked his muzzle.

BEFORE THE DARK COMES, I'D LIKE TO HUNT. WATCH OUR YOUNG, WOULD YOU? She jumped down and went out the door.

Mute crawled into the nest careful not to squash his kittens. They nestled against him and he could feel their tiny bodies rumbling. He would keep them safe and his eyes watched the door. If Algier dared to enter again, he might just have to fight the other until the male was justly defeated.

Much as he appreciated Word Warrior stopping their fight, Mute suspected Algier would not respect the choice Sasha made.

He closed his eyes for quick nap. Part of him stayed alert. His ear twitched and he woke when Sasha returned. She dumped part of a rat on the floor.

They traded places and he ate, properly washing himself afterwards. He watched as Sasha fed their young, washed them, and fell asleep.

Outside night had fallen although it had snowed all day and he suspected it still was. Once again he returned to the computer and was delighted to find a message awaiting him.

HI. I JUST CAME ON DUTY.

Mute wasn't sure what Kat meant. YOU ASKED ABOUT YOUR BROTHER NED. Now why was he bringing that up?

I MISS HIM AND HE'S BEEN GONE FOR SUCH A LONG TIME.

WHERE ARE YOU?

IN A MOUNTAIN.

In a mountain? How could that be?

DO YOU KNOW WHERE NED IS?

His tail wiggled on the counter. Mute didn't actually know Ned, but he knew the fate of the humans in the helicopters. WHERE DO YOU THINK HE IS?

TRUTHFULLY?

He waited.

NED WOULD HAVE COME BACK IF HE WERE STILL ALIVE. AND I HAVE TO THINK HE STILL IS OTHERWISE...

Mute understood loss. He also understood the need to go on. Many died in this harsh land. Just the other day Sasha told him two kittens had been killed by some sort of large predator. The mother hadn't heard a sound. All she'd found had been blood and its bitter scent.

MANY DIE. THAT IS THE WAY OF IT. He hoped Kat understood that.

BUT HOW MANY DIE NEEDLESSLY?

He'd never considered that. His gaze swept over Sasha and their kittens. She'd named the two males Ice and Patch and the female Ara. How would he feel if some predator came in and killed them?

Considering what he'd been prepared to do to Algier, maybe he did understand how Kat felt about her brother.

WHAT WOULD YOU DO IF YOU KNEW HIS FATE? He knew his question might reveal more than he needed to.

I DON'T KNOW. MUTE, DO YOU KNOW SOMETHING YOU'RE NOT TELLING ME?

He did, but he didn't dare endanger Sasha, his kittens or any of the other cats, wolves or snow ghosts.

WHY ARE YOU IN A MOUNTAIN?

THAT'S WHERE OUR ANCESTORS WENT WHEN THE SNOWS CAME.

He still didn't understand how she could live in a mountain. He hadn't read about two-legs living in them. Oh, there'd been references to caves, yet he suspected this wasn't where she lived.

KAT, WHATEVER HAPPED TO YOUR BROTHER, YOU NEED TO KEEP LIVING, TAKE A MATE, AND HAVE YOUNG.

YOU SOUND LIKE OUR LEADERS. UGH

Her response puzzled him. DON'T YOU WANT A MATE OR YOUNG?

OUR LEADERS DECIDE WHO WE MATE WITH. I DON'T LIKE NOT BEING ABLE TO CHOOSE.

His eyes blinked as he considered her words. Sasha had chosen him rather than allow a challenge. So, yes, he could understand why Kat thought that way.

I UNDERSTAND. MY MATE CHOSE ME.

Lucky her.

If you could choose, who would it be?

I don't dare tell you.

Why not?

Just in case someone else find's these messages.

He cocked his head to one side. Why was this two-leg so afraid?

Mute, I have to go. We have teams out and I have to talk with them, if I can, just to make sure they're okay.

What did she mean teams? He'd heard about two-legs visiting the school once. Had they come from the mountain where Kat lived?

We can talk again.

Only at night. No one but me is in the com-center then.

Kat, he hesitated, not sure he was doing the right thing. He'd never known when his foster mother died. He'd known she had since she'd never returned. Do not come looking for Ned. I don't think you'd like what you found. He didn't dare say more than that.

What do you mean?

I can't tell you anything else. Mute ended the messages, turned off the computer and sat on the counter. His tail tip flicked. He sensed he'd said more than he should despite understanding how the two-leg felt. They'd both suffered loss. She deserved to have answers. He just couldn't tell her the full truth.

CHAPTER 15

KAT

What did Mute mean she wouldn't like what she found? Kat puzzled over what her new friend had told her, a cold dread beginning to crawl up her spin. Did he mean Ned was, no, she couldn't think that. She just couldn't!

Kat went through the motions of her duties, scanning the channels and listening for any responses. Even Derrick was mysteriously quiet.

Thinking of the young archeologist made her smile. What would her life be like if she were allowed to choose her own mate, like Sasha had with Mute. Her friend seemed to be happy. Unlike many of the couples she saw in the mountain.

"Quit thinking like that." She tapped her fingers on the counter, completely bored. A soft hiss echoed in the room and Kat really wished she had a way to see outside. Suddenly all the rooms seemed smothering and she felt like she couldn't breathe.

At last her relief arrived and Kat escaped. She grabbed a banana, a tiny orange and some tea from the cafeteria and made her way to the dock. Fish swam by in the water, their mouths briefly showing on the surface before vanishing under the water. The ducks swam all on the far side, and if she saw correctly, they were preening or possibly sleeping.

She peeled her banana and slowly ate it. The orange proved more of a challenge, the sweet juices teasing her taste buds. Kat made a face when she drank her tea. While she'd eaten the beverage had gotten cold.

Something moved and her eyes darted to the side. Slowly creeping toward her was one of the animals a team had brought back. The creature had long black and orange fur, with a heart shaped brown nose. It sniffed the empty peels and made a motion with its paw as if to bury it.

"So what do you eat?"

The creature's ears twitched, before it sat down and licked a spot on its shoulder. When it finished it blinked its yellow eyes.

Tentatively, Kat reached out her fingers. Something moist and wet barely touched them before hissing and backing away.

"You don't have to be like that. Not like I'm gonna hurt you."

With a glare her visitor swished its tail and went to sit on the far edge of the dock. Sometimes its tail thumped against the wood.

A drop of water splashed on Kat's head. She groaned, gathering up her garbage and heading back to her room. Once there she looked around. She ought to be in class, but the thought of sitting through boring useless lessons didn't appeal to her. Not with worry about her brother clawing its way around her brain.

"There has to be something I can do rather than just sitting around hoping he'll contact us."

Kat plopped down on her bunk. Her room seemed much smaller, colder than normal and she wanted to escape. If she left she had no doubt someone would stop her and demand to know why she wasn't in class. She just couldn't deal with that today.

Lying back, Kat tucked the pillow around her head and began to cry. She missed her brother and her parents. Just wasn't fair!

Hours later she awoke. A crazy idea swam in her mind. Their leaders weren't sending out any more search parties. Some lame excuse about not having enough resources and needing to wait until the teams came back in.

Well, Kat decided not to wait. Her brother needed help and she seemed to be the only one who knew. She grabbed some clean clothes and headed for the showers. After she cleaned up, she ventured to the oddly quiet cafeteria. She wandered around picking up fruit and other foods.

Checking to make sure she hadn't been observed Kat returned to her room. She made a couple more trips to the cafeteria, grabbing some tea and some other items she thought she'd need.

After her final trip, she stuffed her stash into pillowcases and hid them under her bed. She carefully packed some extra clothes and knew she'd have to hit the supply room. There were other things she needed.

~ * ~

Several days later, Kat was ready. Luckily, her sister still basically lived in hydroponics, even after they'd fixed the power to their part of the base. No need to worry about her stash being discovered. She'd traded shifts with Tracy who normally worked mornings and then conned Joseph, who worked a few hours every afternoon into covering for her 'for a few days'.

"I need to get in some study time," she'd lied, sealing the deal.

As 'night' fell over the mountain, Kat carefully made several trips to the main auto bay. Nobody was about and only one snow cat remained. She piled her supplies inside and then went into the empty office. Their leaders didn't feel the need to guard the place. After all, who would want to leave?

She rummaged around in the drawer and found the keys. Quickly she checked to make sure it fit before finishing her final supply runs and loading up.

Kat had one last thing she wanted to do. She snuck into the cafeteria and found some stale bread. Cook tended to leave it out for her. Gathering it up, she made a fast trip down to the docks. Water dripped on her head. She didn't care.

The ducks quaked and swam up to her. She tossed the bread out on the water and laughed as they devoured their treat. Even a few fish stole crumbs.

"I'm leaving for a while," she told them as she brushed the last of the crumbs off her hands into the water.

The odd creature she'd seen the other day cocked its head and looked at her.

"I'm going to find my brother." She pointed vaguely to where she knew the entrance was. "Out there."

Rising to its feet, the animal stretched and flicked its tail. Slowly it approached. Kat kneeled down and put out her fingers. Again it sniffed them, but instead of hissing, she felt it lick her.

"Hope you don't think I'm food." She got up and turned to leave, stopping when she realized something had grabbed her. "Now stop that." Kat gently unpeeled the creature's claws. "I have to go while most everyone is asleep."

Kat headed across the deck and headed up the path. When she looked back, she discovered the creature followed her. It stopped when she did, its tail slowly swishing back and forth.

"You should go back." The animal responded by coming closer. Kat gazed into its eyes and flinched. What seemed like intelligence glittered back and for some reason she asked, "Do you want to come with me?"

"Reroow."

"Okay. I'm going to guess that means yes." Kat knelt down. "I'm going to pick you up, so please, don't scratch me." Slowly she got ahold of it and lifted the animal up. She felt its body stiffen before it relaxed. "Okay, let's get out of here."

She hurried up the rest of the path and back to the auto bay. Putting her new friend inside, she crawled in, and started the engine. Luckily, the gas tank was full. She'd made sure of that earlier.

Took her a bit to figure out how to make it work. Slowly the vehicle edged across the garage toward the main door. When she reached it, she stopped, getting out to manually opening it. No doubt someone in the main control room would notice, but glitches were commonplace so maybe they wouldn't send someone to investigate.

Cold and wet snow blasted inside. Kat shivered, re-entered the snow cat and drove outside. She took a moment to manually close the door before making good her escape.

White swirled outside the windshield. Kat swallowed and hoped she didn't inadvertently plunge the snow cat down the side of the mountain. That wouldn't help her brother at all. Not to mention she'd probably freeze to death before help arrived or before she could get back inside the mountain.

Down, down, down she went, the snow cat seeming to crawl the entire time. Dark began to fall and she knew she wanted to be safely at or near the bottom before night fall.

Her unexpected guest had curled up on the seat and she supposed it slept since its eyes were closed.

"Lucky you."

Near the bottom she saw some mounds and hoped maybe they contained structures. She aimed the snow cat toward them and her efforts were rewarded. In the side of one stood a gaping hole. Parking inside as far from the entrance as she could get, she turned off the engine and dug around for the sleeping bag.

Tucking herself inside the thick fabric, she locked the doors and snuggled in for the night. Shuddering sounds surrounded her and Kat hoped they really were safe. Wouldn't do any good if the entire place collapsed and she got buried.

Something bumped her. Her traveling companion looked at her.

"Come on." Kat opened the bag enough to tuck the animal into the warm confines of the sleeping bag. Her companion settled on her lap and its very warm body stopped some of her shivering.

Kat fell into a restless sleep, constantly waking during the night either from the cold or constant noise. When light slowly crept inside, she groaned and unzipped the bag.

"Time to get up," she told her animal.

With a glare its eyes stared at her before deigning to exit and stretch. Claws scratched at the door. "Rerroooo."

"Hope you don't run off on me, although if you do..." Kat shrugged. Unlocking the snow cat, she got out as well looking for a place to relieve herself. She found one in what looked to be an old bathroom. The water didn't work. She washed her hands in snow and looked around.

Torn posters of animals hung haphazardly on the walls. She saw empty shelves and broken tables. A couple places looked like maybe there'd been fire pits, probably from the days when the storms first came. Kat wasn't sure, yet some of it looked like maybe food had once been served here.

"Hey," she called to her companion. "It's getting cold. We need to go."

Her companion reappeared, something small and gray in its mouth. Kat looked away. She knew some animals ate others.

The two got back into the cab and Kat started the engine. "Go ahead and eat, but don't make a mess." Speaking of food, she grabbed a banana and munched on it as she drove out of her night shelter and back onto what must have once been a road.

Skeleton trees poked their heads above the snow, some of the branches ice covered. Old broken power lines had been pulled under the endless white. She could see houses in the distance, their roofs sagged and snapped.

"Huh. Looks like a town."

Spread out before her were the ruins of a good-sized town. Maybe even a city.

"Too bad I don't have time to explore."

Eventually they reached a long road and she followed it north. At least she hoped the old compass she used was right.

"My brother went this way." Her heart sped up a bit. Soon. Soon she'd know what happened to Ned.

CHAPTER 16
WORD WARRIOR

I didn't know the scent outside the school. The entire brick wall reeked, a pungent urine stench burning my nose. I saw dark yellow spots in the snow as well. Huge paw prints headed across the small field and looked like one spot of the old wire fence had been clawed through.

My tail flicked and I wondered if I should follow. If some new predator had decided to make our territory their own, then the kittens coming to learn might be in danger. My eyes followed the path of the intruder. I sniffed again and took a step to follow.

"Word Warrior!" Lara bounded toward me, her black coloring making her easy to see despite some of her white markings. "Word Warrior," she said again as she joined me. "Come quickly."

"What's wrong?"

"It's Callie."

Had I been human I would have used phrase like my heart stopped. A deep fear rose within me as we ran. Our elder had not been well. Indrani had done her best, but the smell of impending death had invaded our home.

Sliding through the window after my mate, I hit the cold carpeted floor. Up the stairs we went to the large room. All my wives were there and they looked at me with fearful eyes.

Starlight sat beside Callie, one delicate paw resting on the old female's leg.

Callie managed to raise her orange head, the scar on her face even more prominent. "Bast is summoning me."

I leapt up and sat beside Starlight. "Do you want to go?"

Our elder closed her eyes and it seemed to take so much effort for her to open them again. "I think…it's time…for my final…sleep."

"Don't go," Starlite begged. "You have so much to teach us yet."

"I've done," Callie panted. "All…that I…can."

Tomura joined us. "You have done well." She licked Callie's

muzzle. "Go and be with Bast. You have earned whatever honor she would bestow upon you."

Lara and Mitzy jumped up, saying their farewells with loving licks.

Callie put her head down on her legs. Once again she closed her eyes. Two more breathes, her tail flicked and her spirit departed.

"Word Warrior." Starlite turned to me. I heard her sadness.

"She is with Bast." While I still did not believe as my wives did, I would not take their hope from them.

"We will clean her," Lara offered.

"Her body can't stay here." I knew the danger.

My first wife offered a solution. "I will ask Rowena to move her body. There is a place she would like and it will keep us safe."

As always, Tomura led. We couldn't have a dead body and growing kittens in the same place. Not only might we fear attack from the butt sniffers who seemed able to devour anything, but it might also attract other predators, like the one I had discovered earlier.

"Thank you." Starlite gave Callie a final lick on her muzzle and then groomed her head.

My other wives helped. When they finished Tomura left us. Not long later Rowena appeared yipping in anguish before releasing a mournful howl. The rest of the pack joined in, their cries echoing through the houses. Vaguely I wondered how far away they could be heard.

Gently Rowena took Callie's body into her powerful mouth. She followed Tomura out the window and into the street. We all trotted behind, down a small hill, down a long path and then into the clear area filled with broken trees. We crossed what the humans called a bridge over a frozen creek.

Rowena placed Callie's body under some thick branches, their green hiding her orange body. Once again the wolf released a mournful howl.

Not far away another wolf howled. I looked up the small rise. Dermot, Rowena's mate, stood there. More howls farther away. No doubt the packs all knew of our loss.

We trudged back in the thick cold snow. We went into our home, all curling together, trying to keep warm and comfort each other.

Rowena and Dermot did not return to their den. Instead, they curled up together on the carpet, the female's head draped over her mate's back.

Slowly, the dark dropped. Starlite nestled next to me. I knew she must be very sad. I had no words to say to her. Instead, I prayed to the Provider.

Nan and Jojo

Jojo lifted his muzzle and howled, pulling Nan from her nap. Further away she heard the mournful sound echoed by the other packs who no longer brought their cubs to be taught.

"What's happened?" she asked her mate.

His sad brown eyes looked down at her. "Callie dead."

"What?" Nan wasn't sure she'd heard correctly.

"Your Elder. Dead."

Pain resonated in her chest. Nan didn't know what to do. Jojo seemed to understand how she felt. He licked her muzzle and his tail thumped a couple of times on the cold floor.

"I'm here."

"I know, Jojo."

More distant howling. One of the packs must be further away hunting.

Nan wanted to run. Where to she didn't know. She controlled her urge knowing it would be dangerous. The large predator they'd seen the other night might be lurking nearby. She had no desire to become a meal for it.

"Nan?" He sniffed her mouth.

She gave his nose a lick, her tongue feeling is warm moistness. She curled tightly, her tail tucked over her nose. Jojo moved and his tail wrapped itself around her. He huffed and she heard his breathing become slow and steady.

It took her longer to fall back to sleep. She would miss Callie.

CHAPTER 17

DERRICK

The com crackled to life. Derrick jumped to answer it hoping it might be Kat.

"Derrick, we have a situation." No such luck. Howard, one of their leaders was calling. The one who usually gave bad news.

"What's going on?" Fear tugged at his belly.

Robert joined him, a curious look on his face.

"Seems Katie Waller took off with our last snow cat a couple of days ago."

The two men exchanged a concerned look.

"She arranged it so we wouldn't discover she was missing until it was too late to stop her."

Robert asked, "Any idea where she's going?"

"Probably to look for her brother in the old city."

Made sense. Derrick knew Kat well enough to know she'd do almost anything to find her older brother. But take the last snow cat when a hunting party might need it? Somehow, that didn't fit.

"You sure one of the hunting parties didn't take it?"

"We're sure." Static crackled and Derrick feared they'd lost the connection. "She took one of those animals Smith's team brought back."

Derrick wondered why.

"We need Katie brought back, along with the animal and the snow cat. Yours is the only team close. Think you can intercept her?"

Derrick looked at the dig with regret. The old store had revealed so much about the culture which had once existed. Even details, or so he assumed, lost on the ruined recordings.

"We can try. You sure she's headed our direction?"

"Coordinates we got from the copters indicated they went north. Our guess she'd do the same."

Knowing the top speed of the snow cat, Derrick was pretty sure Kat had probably reached the city. If the ruins were like the ones they'd been exploring, she could be anywhere in the maze of collapsed buildings and bare trees.

"What do you think, Robert?" He didn't want to make the decision for both of them.

"We can always come back." Robert pointed to the large hole in the ground. "Stopping Katie before she manages to get herself hurt is worth it."

"I agree." He thumbed the com open. "We'll close down the dig and head out in a couple of hours."

"Just make sure you find her and get her back here."

"Will do."

Over the next couple of hours they gathered up their gear and marked the spot with a group of small red flags. He wanted to come back later and finish exploring. They loaded up and headed out.

"Kat doesn't just take off without a reason," Derrick mused, running hand through his dark brown hair.

"From what I remember of the family, they're pretty close." Robert wiggled trying to get more comfortable. He rode in the passenger seat.

"Yeah. They are," Derrick agreed. "I'm just wondering why all of sudden, after months of not hearing from Ned, she'd just leave."

"Think something happened?"

"Hard to say. I know she usually manned the night shift alone."

"Hmmm." Robert scratched his bearded jaw. "Think maybe she got a message from Ned and went looking?"

"I think she would have told me if she had." He clamped his mouth shut. Derrick knew he shouldn't have said that.

His companion sent him a knowing look. "I think you and Kat are bit too close."

"We're friends. Have been since we were children," he defended himself.

"You're not children anymore."

He didn't need to be reminded.

"Doubt our leaders would put you two together."

"I know," Derrick snapped.

"Just remember that."

Yeah, remember that he reminded himself enjoying the heated cab, keeping it just warm enough to enjoy the drive.

Peering out the windshield, Derrick noted the heavy clouds. No doubt they'd have snow dumped on them. Soon.

"Storm coming," Robert commented.

"Saw that."

White flakes fell. He turned on the wipers and lights. The steady drone of the engine filled his ears.

They headed up a hill, take the curves with ease. He wondered if it was an old road they followed.

Robert scratched his stubbled cheek. "If we keep going this way, want to bet it'll take us directly to the old city?"

"We know from the old maps there was a major highway connecting everything."

"Hope we're on it and won't fall through into a building."

"Agreed." Derrick griped the wheel. The snow fell more thickly and the daylight rapidly faded. "Maybe we should stop."

"You can see can't you?"

"Not for much longer."

They crawled down several dips into mini valleys and then climbed out of them. They slowly headed down a slope with what looked like a sharp curve at the bottom.

"There's an old highway sign." Robert pointed.

Overhead waved an old green and white metal sign. Part of it hung downward while the other half bravely tried to hold its ground.

"Can't read it."

"Doesn't matter." Robert straightened in his seat. "Let's follow it."

Turning the wheel they crossed under the sign. At the end were broken poles and to the left what looked like some sort of bridge.

"What do you think?" he asked Robert. "Think that's a good place to spend the night?"

"More protected than most spots we've used."

Maneuvering the snow cat under the broken bridge, Derrick backed up until he almost touched the small hill. Should help block some of the wind. "Hope we don't get snowed in."

Robert chuckled. "Wouldn't be the first time we'd have to dig ourselves out."

Turning off the power, Derrick reached for their sleeping bags while Robert dug out some food. They munched on bread, some nuts and water before crawling into the warm recesses of the fabric.

The cab rocked as wind burst around them. The snow fell so

heavily Derrick could barely see out. He was about to fall asleep when he heard a sound. His heart pounded as it penetrated his very bones and made him freeze, not wanting to move.

CHAPTER 18

KAT

Kat squinted. The storm and thick snow made it difficult for her to see clearly. Vague gray shapes poked out of huge snow drifts. Ahead something crossed the trail she followed. Half of it had broken and she wondered if the missing piece had long ago blown away.

"Urp."

With a nervous glance at her traveling companion, Kat wondered what the creature wanted.

"Not now."

Off to one side stood a huge complex of some sort. Kat searched for a way to reach it since it was blocked by a long wall, now piled high with snow and ice.

"Huh." Her eyes kept looking and finally she found a side way. Or at least she hoped it was. Carefully she guided the snow cat down the narrow path and under what must have once been an overpass, now broken.

The snow cat trudged on and she turned it into a large flat area. Before her sat a huge building. From what she could see the top had long ago caved in.

"Maybe we can find a place to spend the night?"

Her companion ignored her. Licking fur seemed more important.

"Right then."

She noticed a dark hole. Maybe it offered shelter. Kat headed that way.

A gust of wind temporarily blocked her vision. The snow cat rocked. She held her breath afraid the vehicle might turn over. When that didn't happen, she sighed in relief.

A bit later she parked under some sort of structure, which didn't offer as much shelter as she'd hoped. Still, it was better than spending the night out in the open.

"Hungry?" She pulled out some jerky and offered pieces to her companion. The creature nibbled daintily on them and washed itself when it finished eating.

Kat sipped water and ate the dry meat. A little peppery for her taste, but it filled her stomach.

"We'll spend the night here." Grabbing her sleeping bag she slipped inside, opening the top in invitation. "You want to keep warm or not?"

The small warm body on her lap helped and Kat slipped into a restless sleep. The roaring wind woke her several times. When morning finally arrived, she groggily opened her eyes.

With a groan she managed to use a candle to warm a cup of water and make tea. Her companion slipped off her lap and scratched at the door. Kat shivered, but opened it. "Don't go too far."

Breakfast was a muffin and a few pieces of dried fruit. A bit more awake, she looked around. Huge snow drifts piled against the structure almost blocking her exit.

"Maybe I should go exploring." Curious, Kat wondered if she should or go find her brother first. There did seem to be a door not far away. "Oh, why not."

Making sure she had her heaviest coat on, Kat pushed open the door and awkwardly scrambled around the snow. She slipped inside the entrance, the door stuck open by a patch of ice.

Inside, she stopped and gasped. The high ceiling towered above her. Lacing it were wooden beams. All around her chairs and tables, all of them broken, littered the icy floor. And there, dominating the room, a huge rock fireplace stood, its fanciful grills smashed.

"Wow!"

Kat crossed to it. She could tell it had been used in the past by the charred wood inside and dark ashes. How she wished it worked right now!

A scratching sound diverted her attention. Kat took a step back and craned her neck around the corner. Hidden behind a huge table she found more creatures like the one she'd been traveling with. No. Wait a minute. Her companion was there too!

"Friends of yours?"

At being seen, they scrambled and dashed away from her. All except her companion and another slightly larger creature with sandy colored fur and gray stripes.

"What pretty blue eyes you have." She squatted down, reaching out her fingers.

The gray striped animal hissed at her.

A two exchanged a series of chirps and rerows, almost like they were talking. Kat frowned. Now why did she get that impression?

The striped one gave Kat a final snarl and slunk away. The one who had traveled with her, tipped its head and giving her an inquisitive, "Urp?"

"If that's a word, I have no idea what you're saying."

With a graceful swish of the tail, her companion followed the gray striped animal.

"Guess that means I'm on my own." Kat rose, shaking the stiffness out of her legs. "Good luck." She glanced around. "Okay. I think I'll take a look around."

Going further inside the building, she discovered many old stores. Some had once had glass fronts, but they'd been broken long ago. She had to be careful of the icy patches, not wanting to fall. If Kat suffered an injury, she'd have to rescue herself.

"Hard to tell what they once had." Most of the shelves and racks were empty.

She discovered a lower level and Kat went down the metal stairs. The stores were just as empty as the upstairs ones. "Wonder what they used these carts for?" Her gloved fingers ran across one.

In the center she found a frozen lake. Seemed to be man-made and through the ice she could see writing on it. Unfortunately, she couldn't read it.

Going back upstairs she returned to the snow cat. Fluffy white flakes fell thickly. Overhead a bright flash stung her eyes, and immediately thunder shook the building.

Kat shuddered and crawled back into her sleeping bag. She ate a quick lunch of jerky and water. Her eyes refused to stay open and she fell back asleep.

~ * ~

When she awoke again, night had fallen. Kat turned on the lights and gasped. Several drifts had piled around the various pillars. The way she'd come in was blocked!

Not completely she saw, calming her nerves, but enough to make getting out a challenge.

Her stomach rumbled so she rummaged around for something

to eat. Some jerky, a few nuts, and an orange plus water before she turned off the lights and snuggled down in the sleeping bag trying to go back to sleep. The snow cat rocked as wind gusted through.

She really missed her companion. The animal's warmth would have been welcomed. After a time, Kat fell asleep, her dreams filled with images of red tinged snow and growls.

CHAPTER 19
WORD WARRIOR

The fresh fallen snow made it difficult for me to get to the school. I paused several body lengths from our house, my tail slowly swishing. Starlite was very sad and I knew there was little I could do to comfort her after our elder's death. I doubted my wives could either, but they'd decided to stay and at least keep her company.

Callie would be missed. Even by me.

I kept going, my large paws setting an easy pace to travel. I listened for the butt sniffers who often roamed this area. I hadn't seen any for a long while. Not after the wolf pack had killed those that had threatened me and my wives.

I passed a spot smelling of wolf urine. No doubt the pack marking their territory to keep encroachers away. Perhaps it worked well to warn off the butt sniffers as well.

Going down the incline into the school yard, I noticed many females near the entrance. One was yowling and I hurried to find out what had happened.

"Several kittens are dead," Sheba told me.

I looked around for Algier "Where's your mate?"

"He brought home another female just before dark."

Had he challenged and won another?

"She isn't a mate, but you'll want to talk to her."

The yowling female was being groomed by another I knew to be her litter mate.

"What happened?" I asked.

"We don't know." I remembered the female's name was Twillia. "We'd left the kittens to go hunting for rats. When we got back, I could smell their blood."

"There was another smell. Strong. Feline, but not like the Spotted Ghosts," the mourning female added.

A deep anger grew in me. Every kitten was precious. What feline dared invade our dens and kill our young?

"Don't stay in your den. Take a new one."

"We already have." Twillia flicked her tail. "Several of us have gathered in one of the houses to better protect our young."

Why did I get the impression perhaps that was not the best move?

"If you see the predator, send someone to me."

"We will."

Six felines left together, trudging down the hill and into the drainage ditch.

"Come." Sheba led me to the library. Mute sat on the counter, his white head cocked to the side, his paws on the keys. Sasha slept in her nest, her kittens safely by her side.

Algier wasn't there. I hoped he taught his Science class.

Near Sasha's nest a new female slept. Sheba rubbed against the other. Two yellow eyes blinked open. "This is Word Warrior."

"I'm Dia." The female rose, stretched, and sat down, her black and orange tail covering her front paws.

Sheba spoke, "Algier brought Dia here last night. She has a strange tale to tell."

"Humans," Dia began.

Humans? I sat on my haunches and waited for her to continue.

"They live in a mountain."

"How is that possible?" I thought they lived in houses or had in the past.

"I don't know." Dia groomed a spot on her shoulder.

Sheba sat beside the other. Her brown eyes blinked as she listened.

"I came here with one in a metal monster."

The metal monsters we knew well. Kittens and cubs disappeared when they came.

"Where is this human?" Fear grew inside me. Fear for our young. Fear for what could happen if the humans returned and they were as bad as my elder had once told me when I was a kitten.

"I left it at the male gathering place."

Too close. Still a distance of many body lengths yet if it came here…

"Why did it come?"

"I don't know. I didn't understand its language."

Would any of us if we heard a human speak?

CHAPTER 20

DERRICK

They spent an entire day in the snow cat while the storm raged. When finally it cleared, Derrick groaned. Huge drifts had them trapped. "Looks like we're digging our way out."

Robert grunted. He sipped his coffee and munched on some jerky. "Feel good after being trapped in here."

Derrick chuckled. He had to agree. Stretching his muscles would feel good after being cramped inside for as long as they'd been.

After breakfast they each grabbed a shovel and began digging. Freeing the snow cat took several hours so they could leave their temporary shelter and continue on.

"Any idea where Katie would have headed?" Robert asked.

"Not clearly." Derrick crawled back inside and thumbed the mic. "This is Derrick Metcalf to base. Come in base."

Static answered and he shivered as Robert closed his door.

"This is base over." He recognized Olga's voice.

"Do we have any coordinates from Ned Waller's last known position?"

Derrick knew it was a long shot, but it was his best guess. At least it would give him a starting point.

His question caused a long silence. Maybe they'd lost their connection. Then Olga spoke again. She spouted off a set of numbers. Thankfully, Robert wrote them down.

"Got it. Thanks."

"Just bring that little troublemaker back so I can tell her how stupid she's being."

Olga grumped a few more words Derrick chose to ignore.

Robert was already figuring out where they needed to go. "Northwest for a couple of miles."

Derrick nodded. "Signing off." He turned off the com. "Let's get going."

He headed the snow cat in the right direction. They passed a huge building which must have been, from what little of the sign he could read, a hospital.

Robert said, "We should stop and see if there's anything we could use."

"Maybe on the way back."

The other man glared at him and looked out the window.

They passed other buildings, many of them buckling under the weight of ice and snow. Derrick headed north since there didn't seem to be any way to get directly to their destination. The snow cat crawled up an incline. At the crest it went down again. In the distance stood a huge structure.

"Love to explore that," Derrick commented.

"Next trip." Robert settled back in the creaking seat.

Heading west they passed a large open area with bare white trees. Something moved and Derrick sat forward trying to make it out.

"Just an animal." Robert was busy checking their position.

"Think we should capture it?"

"Naw. Let another team do that."

He watched as the animal seemed to be following them by dodging behind trees or snow mounds. Was it trying to hide from them?

Shaking his head Derrick kept going. Ahead something hung in the air and swayed back and forth in the wind. He crossed under it a little uneasy. Knowing it would do major damage if the metal snapped and fell.

They passed more buildings and more dead trees until they found a passage with several structures sitting on various corners. Turning north, he slowly edged across an overpass, more than a little nervous. There had been years of snow and ice pressure on it. Would it hold their weight?

He held his breath as they crossed, terrified, although he'd never admit his fear to Robert. Images of the structure buckling and sending them in to the deep drift haunted him.

When they got to the other side, he took a deep breath. "Now which way?"

Robert consulted his map. "Just a bit further north than west."

The snow cat plodded along, leaving large prints in the new fallen snow. Robert turned west and stopped.

"Oh, my, god."

CHAPTER 21

KAT

Sun glittered on the snow piercing under the structure and prying at Kat's eyelids. She groaned. Slowly she emerged from her warm sleeping bag, ducking outside to relieve herself before warming water for tea. She cupped the mug allowing the heat to chase away the last of the chill.

As she munched on some nuts, Kat looked around. High mounds of snow almost closed off her exit. Not that she doubted she could get out. The snow cats had been built sturdy and reliable, or so Ned had always told her. Beyond her shelter she could see the roofs of other buildings.

"Derrick would love this." Even thinking of the young archeologist made her blush. Quickly she finished her breakfast before digging out her notes. Her brother's last reported position was maybe about a mile or two from where she currently sat. She'd be there in no time.

The engine rumbled awake and passed between the pillars back outside. The treads easily rolled over the new snow and she set her course. Keeping an eye on the compass she enjoyed the endless white. Here and there things poked out of it. A clump of dead trees, a broken roof, other things she'd only seen pictures of.

Her path was pretty much unobstructed. Maybe she followed an old road. Good. Kat wouldn't have to worry about running over anything.

A few minutes later she turned north. Her foot slammed down on the brake. Impressed in the snow she saw the tracks of another snow cat. What should she do?

As she watched two figures got out. They wore the ugly green and they had their hoods up. Yet something about the way one of them moved seemed familiar to her.

"Oh, it can't be." What would Derrick be doing here? Kat tapped her fingers on the steering wheel debating what to do. Were they searching for her? Or had Derrick simply decided to go exploring further north? Only one way to find out she decided.

Moving the machine forward she angled her snow cat to stop beside theirs. She opened the door and waved. "Hi, guys."

"You are in so much trouble, young lady," Robert scolded her.

"Hey, Kat," Derrick greeted. He glanced uneasily over his shoulder.

"So, what are you two doing here?" She slid out of her seat and stood beside Derrick. He moved so she couldn't see beyond him.

"Looking for you," Robert responded. "You know better than to take off with the last snow cat. What if they needed to go hunting?"

She snorted. He knew as well as she did most of the hunting parties went out on foot. "They sent you after me didn't they?"

"They did." Derrick lightly touched her arm. "Kat, you really shouldn't have taken off like you did."

"I wanted to find Ned."

Robert glared at her. "He isn't here."

"You don't mind if I see for myself." Kat pushed past Derrick and stared at what he'd been trying to hide. Pieces of scorched metal stuck out from under the snow. And were her eyes playing tricks on her or were there splotches of red peeking through the fresh snow? They resembled what she'd seen in her nightmares.

Derrick made a grab for her. She pushed him away. Kat ran toward the wreckage, or the best she could manage through the deep snow. She stopped, her breath coming in ragged sobs.

"I wanted to spare you this." Derrick stood beside her.

Her cheeks grew cold as her tears froze on her face. "What did you find?"

"Nothing yet. Just wreckage."

"If he was here," she managed. "I have to know."

Derrick glanced back at his companion. "We'll do what we can."

"Good." She trudged back to her snow cat. "Robert, where do you think would make a good place to camp?"

The older man pursed his lips and shook his head. He started to speak, but Derrick cut him off. "How about the old store?"

Robert glanced at the structure. "Looks like it might collapse at any moment."

Kat pointed at a brick structure near them. "What about that one?"

"Might do."

They parked the snow cats just outside, taking their camping gear in. The shelves were empty. Robert put down a clay pot and started a fire.

"What's that?" Kat gazed at it curious.

"Took it from our dig. Kept us warm."

A flame danced up and licked the side. Robert put more fuel on it and soon a warm blaze warmed the area. While it kept some of the cold at bay, the building was large and Kat shivered.

"Tomorrow," Derrick said as he warmed some water. "We'll dig through some of the wreckage. See what we find."

"Should check in." Robert started accusingly at Derrick.

"Go ahead."

"And if they order us back?"

"Tell them what we found and ask if they'll give us a few days."

"Leaders aren't going to like that."

"We're a long way from the mountain."

Robert narrowed his brown eyes. "Not a wise move."

"Robert, we need to know."

Shaking his head the older man left.

"I don't want to get you into trouble." Kat felt guilty Derrick seemed willing to help her.

"We had too many teams just vanish. If we can find out the fate of at least one, we'll know more than we did."

Kat understood that. She was just terrified of what they'd find. Derrick handed her a cup and she made tea. The hot liquid helped calm her shivering body.

"Might want to crawl into your sleeping bag." Derrick spread his out near the warming pot.

She put down her mug and did the same, crawling in to help keep her body warm.

Robert returned grumbling. "They don't like it, but they agreed with you."

Derrick smiled his face lighting up. Kat glanced down trying to keep her interest in the young man a secret.

They shared a meal of jerky, nuts and the last of Kat's oranges. Dark dropped over them, the fire not able to keep it at bay.

"Might as well sleep, Katie." Robert rolled into his bag, putting his back to the fire.

"He's right," Derrick agreed as he did the same.

Kat sat there for a long while, listening to the two men breathe. In the distance she heard howling and she pulled her bag tighter around her body. From further away came more howling.

She whispered, "You just stay out there and away from us."

~ * ~

After breakfast Kat joined the two men outside. They had part of the helicopter unburied and something lumpy under a tarp. She squeezed her eyes closed afraid of what it might be.

"Found a body," Robert said. He paused to wipe sweat off his forehead.

"Know whose?"

"Not until we get it back to the mountain."

Kat braced herself and went to pull away the covering.

"Kat," Derrick's voice stopped her. "It's burned very badly. You don't want to see it."

She nodded and backed away. "What can I do to help?"

Derrick pointed to the surrounding area. "See what else you can find without having to dig."

"Okay." She moved a little ways away from the men, her eyes searching the ground. Kat found tracks, some large and a few smaller ones. Probably some kind of animal with its young if the training she'd gotten was any good.

Moving slowly across the mostly open expanse, there were a few bare trees here and there, she managed to get to the far side. Most of the buildings had been smashed under the snow's weight.

She lifted a hand to shield her eyes. In the distance an odd blue and white structure caught her attention. Very far away she saw more mountains. They stood proud and white covered, billowy clouds rushing across the gray sky. What would it be like to reach them and then keep going? What would she find?

With a wistful sigh, she returned to the men. Her eyes caught a movement and she froze, afraid to move or even to scream.

Two figures darted around a corner, stopping to observe the activity. One looked like her companion while the other was more canine, much like some of the creatures a couple of teams had brought back and attempted to train.

The two stood there for a long while before finally moving around a corner and vanishing.

Kat couldn't stop herself. She hurried across the distance, ducking around the corner to see where they'd gone. The odd pair moved quickly in what she was sure a south easterly direction.

Part of her wanted to track them while the other part warned her against such folly. She was here to discover what happened to her brother, not worry about what two animals were doing. Besides, they might easily turn on her and she'd become prey. Kat had no desire to share her parent's fate.

She reached the site to find the two men munching on jerky. Come to think of it, she was hungry. Kat hurried to their camp and made lunch for herself and rejoined the others afterward.

"Found another body," Derrick informed her.

"My brother?"

"Can't tell. Badly burned."

Kat tried to hide her disappointment. With nothing else to do she wandered around the area, picking up small pieces of debris and putting them into a bag. Her hand brushed against something and she jumped back. Carefully she knelt down and dug with round it.

"Oh, you poor thing." A lump formed in her throat at the sight of a young canine trapped in a net. The head sat at an odd angle and from the muzzle dried blood had dripped staining the snow. "Hey, Derrick!"

He dropped his shovel and joined her. "What did you find?"

"Look."

Derrick looked at the body. "Wonder how this happened."

"Guess we'll never know."

"Not unless we find a survivor." He sat back on his heels. "From what we're finding in the wreckage seems highly doubtful." His eyes looked at Kat. They held both sympathy and sadness. "I think you're going to have accept the fact Ned is dead."

Kat gulped and shook her head. "I can't."

Derrick took a deep breath. "No one could have survived the crash."

"If Ned could, he would." She got up. "We should bury this poor creature."

"Ground is too hard."

She knew he was right. "I'm sorry," she told the animal.

Derrick looked at her strangely. "Come on, Kat. It's just an animal."

Kat nodded. "I'm going back to camp."

"Be there shortly." He glanced at the sky. "Night's coming soon."

Making her way back through the snow, Kat fought her sadness and disappointment. She was not going to cry. She was not!

She dumped more fuel on the fire and began to warm water. The men would need a hot drink when they got back. Kat also rummaged through the supplies to see what they had to eat. Munching on jerky, nuts and fruit was okay when on the move, but they needed something more nourishing.

In a box she found a few vegetables and a large pot. She poured the hot water over them and broke up some of jerky for a broth. Setting in across the fire, she warmed more water for tea.

The shadows grew long and the wind began to blow. Kat tucked her sleeping bag around her and stirred the soup, enjoying the enticing aroma.

Warming her hands over the flames she waited for Derrick and Robert. She heard their tromping feet and smiled. They'd both be pleased, or so she hoped, with her surprise.

"What smells so good?" Derrick smiled at her.

"Figured soup would be good."

"Huh." Robert sat down, helping himself.

They ate in silence as the wind rattled the glass and Kat heard something snap.

"Probably a tree," Derrick commented as he sipped the soup.

The room got even darker. Their cozy fire crackled, and Kat found herself getting drowsy. "Night," she mumbled.

"Night," the two men replied.

Vaguely she heard the howling. Since the owners of the sound hadn't bothered them the night before, she ignored the sounds.

At some point she awoke. Other than the embers of the fire the room was pitch black. She heard a huffing sound and a high-pitched squeal, followed by a growling she'd never heard before. One that echoed in her bones and scared her so badly she couldn't move.

"Derrick," she whispered. He didn't answer. "Derrick?" she tried again a bit more loudly.

"Don't move and be quiet."

She pretended she was one of mice she'd sometimes see around the pond. Quiet and still. Not prey.

She heard something moving behind her. Kat didn't dare move.

A long time later, something touched her shoulder and she jumped. "It's just me," Derrick reassured her.

"What was it?"

"No idea. Tracks were huge."

She turned toward the fire. Robert was sitting up, a gun in his hand. Derrick squatted next to her. "It couldn't get in so it scratched the glass."

"Was it a bear?"

Robert spoke up. "No. Definitely a large predator though. We're going to want to keep an eye out."

"We didn't see it today. Maybe it only hunts at night?" Kat certainly hoped that was the case.

"Maybe." Robert put some fuel on the fire. "You two go back to sleep. I'll take first watch."

Kat curled back into her sleeping bag. She heard Derrick do the same. The fire sizzled. The sound soothed her being both familiar and friendly.

At some point she fell asleep, her dreams filled with large animals hunting her, and smaller ones talking to her.

CHAPTER 22

MUTE

Disappointed, Mute turned off the email. He'd sent several messages, but Kat had not responded. His tail flicked and he felt the cold countertop through his paws. Sasha nursed their kittens. They were growing fast and soon they'd be attending their first reading class.

He glanced up as something moved by the door, relaxing as he recognized Word Warrior. The dominant male cat posed no threat to him, his mate or their young.

Two others joined the male. Jojo and Nan. He wondered why they were here and not their new den. From what his mate had told him, the pair watched for any threat from the two-legs. Maybe their presence here suggested some new development.

He had no way to know unless someone typed on the computer screen and told him. His neck itched and he raised his hind leg trying to ease the irritation. He cleaned a place on his belly before hopping down.

Sasha now washed their young. One of them edged out of the nest. Mute caught the youngster by the neck and returned the kitten to his mother. She licked Mute's muzzle in thanks.

Looking toward the door again he watched Nan, Jojo and Word Warrior. They were all sitting, not moving other than their tails. The wolf's was stirring up dust.

He sneezed and returned to the computer. Maybe Kat had responded. Mute wasn't sure what he was going to do if he never heard from her again.

Or maybe he should tell Word Warrior about his unmet friend who he thought could be human. Or maybe he shouldn't since he didn't know for sure.

Mute sat staring at the screen waiting for any message at all, disappointed when none came. Finally he jumped down and joined Sasha in the nest helping to keep their kittens warm. At least he could do that much.

Maybe later he'd talk to Word Warrior. His kitten's safety was far more important than a threat that might or might not exist.

WORD WARRIOR

"You're sure about what you saw?" I asked.

"Yes," Nan answered. "There are two metal monsters where the helicopters burned."

"And two-legs," Jojo added.

Two-legs, probably humans. I wasn't sure what to do about them except maybe go see them. We'd have to be careful. I had no idea why they'd returned, but I doubted it would be good for us.

"Has any wolf told of a missing cub or the females a missing kitten?" That was my first concern.

"None." Nan's tan tail settled over her paws. Again I marveled how much she looked like her mother Tomura.

Jojo growled. No doubt defending his pack. Rowena and Dermot would soon have pups.

"I will come and see them."

"Do you think that's wise father?" Nan gazed at me with her yellow eyes. "We don't really know why they're here."

"My guess," and I was only speculating. "Is that they came to find out what happened to the two-legs who burned in the crashes."

"What if they found the dead cub?" Nan looked at Jojo. "What if they blame us? The packs were terrified of what would happen."

I was too. I remembered how most of the wolves left us except for Lavena's and Rowena's packs. When the other packs had killed the two-legs for the death of a cub, the fear had grown. None of their pups had come back to school.

I got to my paws. I was the leader here. I needed to see them.

"You should tell my mother," Nan told me.

"Your mother is with my other wives. They stayed at our den."

"They haven't come back to teach yet?"

"Starlite is very sad." I hoped she would soon not be. The kittens needed their teachers.

"You ready Jojo?" Nan got up and stretched her back.

"Go." Jojo sprang up and padded down the cold hallway.

I followed the wolf my daughter walking beside me.

Blythe and Ellen dashed in. I stopped admiring them. They'd grown into fine females who would no doubt soon find mates.

"Is it true?" Ellen asked. Her black spots shone attractively against her gray fur.

"Is what true?" I asked.

"Is she here?" Blythe demanded. Her coloring was the opposite of her sister's.

"Is who here?" I had no idea whom they spoke of.

"Our mother." Ellen sneezed from the dust Jojo's tail was making.

Their mother?

Nan blinked her eyes. "Who's your mother?"

Before either could answer, the female who told me about traveling with the two-leg darted into the corridor. She saw the two sisters and ran toward them. They all bumped sides and touched noses, their purrs echoing.

"Dia is your mother?" I had no idea.

"Yes," Blythe replied.

"Mother where have you been?" Ellen wanted to know.

"In a mountain."

I still wanted to know how she could have been inside a mountain.

"Tell us all about it." The two waited expectantly.

Algier stood in a door where he held his Science class. "Could you all be quiet. We're learning about the solar system today and it's difficult for my students to comprehend."

"Sorry," Dia apologized. "I just found my daughters."

The male spat and went back to his class.

"Come mother, we have a nice den. You can stay with us." The three females left, talking constantly.

"That's wonderful!" Nan's tail flicked.

Jojo yipped and darted outside. He must have agreed with my daughter.

"How do you like your new den?" I asked as we followed the wolf.

"It has strange things along the walls and I don't know what they are."

"I trust it keeps out the snow."

"The lower levels do. Not the upper ones."

We traveled down the hill and toward one of the underground pipes. Jojo went ahead of us, sniffing the ground. His tail kept wagging.

I was thankful to be out of the cold wind. Only part of the way could we travel underground. The rest we'd be exposed.

Jojo stopped. I heard his deep throated growl.

Nan hopped ahead. "What's wrong?"

"Stay behind me." He stepped protectively in front of my daughter.

I moved to his side. Here I could smell the strong stench of urine. My fur puffed up and I hissed, warning the intruder I was ready for battle.

A roar answered us. Two large yellow eyes appeared attached to a massive head covered in white fur and black strips. The feline's claws were the largest I'd seen and the very long tail twitched violently.

My nose filled with the reek of blood and rank meat. A dead deer lay across our path and its killer blocked out way.

A large paw raked at us. Both Jojo and I jumped back. I had thought the Snow Ghosts large!

"Nan, go," I ordered. "Slowly. Don't run." How had I known to tell her that?

"Father,"

"Slowly. Don't turn around. Keep watching."

She obeyed. Jojo and I backed away, not daring to turn around until we could no longer see the predator.

As we retreated I remembered the urine smell since I'd found on the school wall. Now I knew what type of cat had made it and feared we had a new danger facing us.

~ * ~

Back in the open we headed down the small valley. Snow began to fall. I would have preferred to travel underground, but not with a new threat. Luckily, it had not followed us. I hoped it was too hungry and afraid to leave its kill.

We passed the huge building the Snow Ghosts had made their new home. Part of the building had collapsed. Indrani had told me about it. We crossed the small clearing and headed behind another large structure. Long ago it had broken wood and concrete jutting up like bones.

Past it was more buildings. What had the humans used all of these for?

We came to the crossover place, an overpass they'd once been called. I could see the large metal monster tracks.

"Smell funny." Jojo pulled his nose out of one and sneezed. "Not living."

"I wonder what they are," Nan mused.

We kept going despite the gathering storm. Wind gusted around us, sometimes swirling so hard it was difficult to see.

"There!" Nan dashed ahead.

Vaguely I could see what excited her. Two odd machines parked outside one of the buildings.

Jojo stopped a few body lengths away. He snarled.

I caught the scent too. The same strong urine odor.

Nan stood by the window. She peered inside. I joined her.

Inside a flame flickered. Instinctively I was afraid. We all knew that fire could destroy. Yet it seemed to be contained and controlled. How could that be?

A figure moved around it and I could smell different scents unfamiliar to me.

Jojo yipped a warning and we moved away from the window, hiding behind one of the machines. Two more figures emerged from the storm and stumbled inside.

Curious I crept back, my belly rubbing against the whirling white. I wanted to be as small as possible so they wouldn't see me.

Vaguely I heard strange sounds. I had no idea what they were doing.

When the cold snow drizzled down my back, I knew it was time to go. I rejoined Nan and Jojo. My daughter had curled tightly against the wolf's side.

"Do we have to travel back to the school?" Nan asked.

"No." Even I knew it would be too dangerous. Not only from the cold, but both Nan and Jojo's fur dripped with snow. Not far away was another building. If we could get there, we could stay until the storm stopped.

I led the way. It seemed to take forever and my body was very, very cold by the time we reached our destination. Crawling through a small open space, we entered the place. I saw shelves everywhere and some items scattered on the floor. Jojo sniffed and headed toward the back.

Nan shivered. "I'm cold."

As was I.

The wolf came back dragging a large fur covered coat. He dropped it in a sheltered area, curling up to claim his spot. Nan began drying herself and I did the same.

Once dry, I claimed a place for myself. Nan once again curled up against the wolf. His tail dropped protectively in front of her.

The wind caused the building to shake and groan. I closed my eyes trying to ignore it. Dark fell. In the distance I could hear the packs howling. What were they doing out in a storm like this?

Jojo howled in return. I lifted my head. "What's going on?"

"Two pups dead."

"How?"

"Stinky predator."

A chill not born of the storm touched me. Several kittens had been killed. Was this new predator the cause? And if so, what was I going to do about it?

CHAPTER 23

SITA

Sita could not believe the foolishness of these creatures. They lived so close together their scents proved easy to track. Fortunate for her and the cubs she carried. Plentiful prey would keep her well-fed.

She stretched her large body, rubbing her back on the cold ground. The unevenness made it simple to scratch an annoying patch along her spine. Ahhh. That was better.

Her long, striped tail flicked, beating against the rock-like surface. She'd found the perfect lair. Not far away something dripped meaning she had drinking water. The prey she'd brought down was almost gone and eventually, after she took a nap, she would go hunting again.

One of cubs punched her stomach. By the next full moon they'd arrive. She'd be plenty busy caring for them.

She licked blood from her paw, using it to clean behind her ear. Sita was proud of her white body and beautiful stripes. Keeping it clean took time, but considering the mate she'd attracted, her efforts had been well worth it.

The howling started again. She paused in her washing to listen. Her ear twitched. Those were harder to catch. Good eating though as long as she did not get bitten very much. She'd seen others of her kind die from them.

Other than the ponderers, the strange beasts who could ramble the land on four legs, but could stand on two, she was the strongest predator.

Her washing done, she laid back and took a well-deserved nap.

When Sita woke, she stretched, allowing her strong hunting muscles to flex. She would need them later. Padding to the entrance she stared out on a land being covered yet again in the cold white stuff. Not that she really minded, but deep in her memory she shared the knowledge about a place of warmth and water she could swim in. The memory wasn't hers and she couldn't remember her mother telling her about it, yet it remained.

Small forms moved in the storm. They scrambled up the hill and headed for the large stone thing she'd marked for her own. Curious, she followed, keeping low so they would not see her.

They entered her claimed domain. Her nose told her there were many there. Maybe later she'd explore it. For now, her gaze turned to the smaller more wooden things. A female howling thing exited. She could see the distended tits and knew this one had given birth.

Her mouth began to water. Young were easy prey. She waited until the other had gone into the stone place before creeping toward her prey. Her paws mounted the odd hill and she stuck her great head into the opening.

Tiny yips greeted her ears. She brushed the cold ground with her stomach as she slowly stalked them. Pausing, ready to pounce, she vaguely saw a shadow.

Low growling stopped her. She swung her head toward the sound. A young howling thing guarded the young, his teeth bared.

She snarled. That was usually enough to scare one away.

The young one didn't move. He released a loud howl and lunged at her. She could easily have swatted him aside, but his attack surprised her. These same creatures when she encountered them in the mountains ran from her. Why did this one attack?

Teeth closed on her tail. She whirled around. The female had returned and behind her snarled two more. They attacked. Sita knew she was trapped. She roared and heard a yelp as her claws found flesh. Blood smell filled her nose.

Desperate she launched her body for the door. She missed the small hill and landed awkwardly in the snow. Floundering to her feet she dashed away, through small forms that scattered and yowled. Down the hill she fled and away from her lair. No need to lead them to her future birthing place.

On and on she ran, finally taking refuge in another stone cave. There, she washed herself, taking great care to tend her wounds.

A cub stepped on her stomach and she growled at it.

When she finished she curled up and took a nap. Rest would help her heal.

Then, she would hunt again.

DERMOT

"Rowena! The pups!"

His mate dashed to them. Her three pups yipped. "They're fine."

Dermot turned his attention to Iden. "Well done."

The young male licked at a dripping wound. "I did my best."

"You saved them," Rowena reassured him. "Otherwise, they'd be prey now."

Dermot came closer to examine Iden's wound. "You should go see Indrani." He turned to the female behind him. "Thank you for your help Cara."

She growled. "Pups are not prey."

Normally no. He knew in the mountains they could be. Many pups had been lost to predators or because they wandered too far from the den and died from the cold.

He turned to his mate. "Should we move them?"

Rowena glanced from her cubs to her mate. He could see her instincts battling with each other as a lesser wolf might with the dominate for control.

"Yes." She took one by the neck. He took another and Cara dared to take the third. The pack exited the building and trotted across the ground toward the school.

Tomura rushed out. "I was just told what happened."

Iden spoke carefully around the small body he carried. "We need to move the pups."

"We may need to move all of us," Starlite said, her blue eyes not really seeing them. "The predator will return."

Tomura glanced at the other. "What do you see?"

"Blood and bodies everywhere."

"Come," Tomura directed. "You'll stay in our den."

"Iden," Starlite looked at the young wolf. "Go to Indrani."

The wolf hesitated then limped down the hill toward the large structure many body lengths away.

Dermot and the two females followed Tomura and Starlite to their den. He knew they'd long ago left the school. They entered the new den through an open window.

"There's a room there." Tomura showed them the door. "With its own window so you may enter and leave without being seen."

Rowena placed the pup she carried on a heavy coat. Dermot

could smell the other cats who lived there. He put down his pup as did Cara. Immediately his mate joined her pups and they grabbed her tits.

Cara looked longingly at the pups and leapt out the window. He knew she wanted pups too. Unfortunately, she'd given up her place as the dominate even though she'd challenged Rowena and lost.

"She'll be fine," Rowena reassured him.

He had to admit he loved Rowena's thick white fur. He yipped softly and went back to where the cats waited. "They're eating."

"As all young should." Tomura sat regally, her thin tan tail tucked over her claws.

Starlite gazed out the window. "The predator will return."

"And we'll be ready for it," Dermot vowed. "Our pups will not be rightful prey."

CHAPTER 24

KAT

She spotted tracks outside the building. They seemed to lead across the street and vanished into another building. Kat blew on her chilled fingers and wondered what type of animals had visited them.

The cold creeping through the glass drove her back to the fire. She gingerly opened her hands over the heat and sighed as her fingers warmed.

"Talked to the mountain last night." She glanced up as Derrick squatted down. "They're insisting we return as soon as possible."

"Did you tell them what we found?"

He nodded, his breath making a small cloud in front of his face. "Told them we'd be a few more days."

"What did they say?"

"Nothing you want to hear." He picked up his mug and poured hot water in it. Adding a few leaves he said, "I don't think our leaders honestly wanted to know what happened to either copter mission."

"Why?" Kat didn't expect Derrick to know the answer.

"Could be a lot of reasons." He sipped his brew. "We found the second one."

Kat caught her breath almost afraid to ask. "And?"

"Still intact." He took a drink. "One body. So far."

Kat could tell he hadn't told her everything from his taut face. "Where's Robert?"

"Got up just before dawn." He took a couple more swigs. "Wanted to take a look around before we started digging again today."

"Surprised you haven't gone through the other buildings yet." Her mind drifted to the animal tracks.

"Maybe next trip." Derrick finished his drink, stood up and stretched. "I'm going out to dig. Stay out of trouble." He winked and trotted out of the building. The brief breeze made Kat shiver.

She had a quick breakfast of nuts and dried fruit along with a cup of tea. She again drifted to window and started out at the tracks.

Maybe I should see where they go.

Before she could act on her thought, three animals came out of the building. She couldn't see them clearly, just blurry shapes. Dashing out the door she stumbled up the incline and tried to get a better look.

Browns and blacks met her eyes. They turned away from her and headed the same way she and the men had arrived. The wind gusted blocking her view. When it cleared she could no longer see the creatures.

"I wonder where they were going," she murmured.

Not wanting to go back inside, she trudged to where the two men dug. Most of the second copter had been uncovered. Twisted metal and fragments littered the ground. Not far away a tarp covered a shape.

"Don't look, Kat," Derrick warned.

"Who is it?" She was almost afraid of the answer.

"Not sure. There's damage." He didn't go into detail. Kat wasn't sure if she wanted to know.

"I found a dead baby animal the other day." Kat volunteered, not sure why she shared it. Derrick already knew.

Derrick nodded and kept digging.

Kat saw Robert on the other side of the helicopter where he'd spread another tarp. She swallowed. "I'm going back to camp."

Her friend grunted. She sighed and worked her way back. Once there she added more fuel to the fire and wondered if they had enough supplies for another soup. They did although she could see they'd have to soon return to the mountain.

Kat didn't know if she wanted to return.

DERRICK

"You didn't tell her," Robert accused.

Derrick didn't stop clearing snow. "She doesn't need to know yet. Besides, until the remains are identified, we can't be sure."

Robert didn't say anything more. They worked in companionable silence broken only by the wind.

The temperature got colder and Derrick knew they needed to head back. "Time to go."

"Agreed."

They picked up their equipment and returned to camp. When Derrick opened the door his nose filled with a wonderful scent. "Made soup again?"

Kat smiled at him. His heart sped up even as he tried to squash the feelings he had for her.

Robert spared him a glance before going to stand before the fire. Derrick wiped off as much snow as possible before joining the others. He extended his hands over the flame. "Feels good."

"I'm surprised you two stayed out as long as you did." Kat smiled teasingly at them. "Don't you remember our survival classes?"

Derrick returned her smile. "Only too well."

Robert chuckled. "Smells good, Katie. Thanks for cooking for us."

"You're welcome." She poured the food into tin cups and drank some of hers. "I saw three animals today."

Derrick and Robert shared a look. They knew what the bodies they'd found looked like. Not all of the damage happened during the crash.

"They come near you?" Derrick asked concerned.

"No." Her eyes met his. "They did look through the window at us."

That startled him. Most of the animals ran. "Where did you see them?"

"Coming out of the other building." She pointed in the general direction. "They took off the direction we came. I lost them thanks to the wind."

Probably a good thing. Derrick hated to think of what they might do to her. "Good thing you didn't go after them."

"Like I said, I lost them. Besides, it was too cold."

They finished dinner while the wind banged against the window. Kat scrubbed their cups clean with snow and then settled into her sleeping bag. He knew from her breathing she'd fallen asleep.

Robert started to speak. Derrick shook his head. His companion nodded his understanding.

After adding more fuel, Derrick crawled into his sleeping bag. Robert stayed up scribbling notes. When he finally heard the zip of the bag, Derrick relaxed and allowed himself to drift off.

Vaguely in the distance he heard howling cut off by a sharp roar.

He sat up, his heart pounding. When no sounds followed, he

forced himself to lie down again.

Took a very long while before he relaxed enough to sleep.

KAT

From the constant rustles, Kat could tell how restless Derrick was. She tried to be still, slowly rolling on her back as if doing so asleep. Opening her eyes, she watched the shadows play over the frozen ceiling. The way they moved they reminded her of the ghost stories she'd heard growing up. Never mind it was just the flickering fire playing tricks on her.

She inched a bit closer to their fire. Didn't seem which way she turned a part of her always got cold. A shiver worked its way up her body. She groaned and then wished she hadn't. What if Derrick had heard her?

"You okay?"

Drat. He had. "Fine," she answered. "Just a bit cold."

The wind rattled some object outside. Another shiver shook her body.

"Move closer to the fire. That should help."

With a sigh she managed to get closer while not actually getting out of her sleeping bag. The heat played over the fabric making it a bit warmer.

"Go to sleep, Kat."

"I'll try."

Silence followed. The flames continued to cast shadows on the ceiling. All around her figures seemed to run along the shelves only to vanish down long dark halls.

What had this place been like? What had filled it and had people come here? If so, what for? Nothing she saw gave any hint about what its function had once been.

Warmth slowly settled over her making Kat drowsy. Hoping she could sleep, her eyes darted to the window. A large shape passed by and she heard a high pitched screech.

Terrified, she couldn't move. Couldn't even call for Derrick.

More roars sounded like nothing she'd never heard and she screamed.

DERRICK

Kat's terror shredded Derrick's sleep. He jumped out of his sleeping bag, his hand reaching for the nearest weapon, closing on the shovel handle. Holding it before him, he advanced toward the door.

A rustling noise behind him informed him Robert was also up.

"Careful," the older man warned. "We don't know what we're dealing with."

They reached the entrance and stopped. Outside a huge predator, much like some smaller creatures that had been brought back. A deep growl came out of its mouth and a large paw swiped at the door, clearly frustrated.

"Look at those claws," Robert marveled. "Probably hunts."

"Us?" Kat stood behind them.

"Can't get to us," Robert reassured her. "Otherwise, we'd all be dead."

Derrick knew Robert was right and hated the words had said in front of Kat. One glance at her terrified face made him want to protect her.

The animal paced several times making frustrated snarls and growls.

"Where's the rifle?" Derrick asked.

"In the snow cat."

"Good place for it."

Robert threw him a 'yeah, I know' look. "Didn't really figure we'd need it."

He couldn't disagree. Other than the incident which had killed the others in their party, they really hadn't encountered anything deadly.

Until now.

KAT

The large predator outside eyed them hungrily. Claws worked at the door again and Kat took a step back. "You sure it can't get in?"

"Hasn't yet," Robert replied. He looked around. "Come on, Derrick. Let's move some of this shelving against the door."

Derrick looked doubtful. He handed the shovel to Kat.

Her eyes glanced at the shovel. "What am I supposed to do with this?"

"Just hold it," he snapped back.

She watched as the two men knocked over one of the racks and pushed it in front of the door.

"You're really sure that's going to keep it out?" Somehow she doubted it.

Derrick took the shovel. Restlessly he turned the handle in his roughened hands.

"Let's get back to the fire," Robert suggested. "I think it will help."

"Hope so," she mumbled. The cold began to seep through and she crawled back in her sleeping bag. Instead of lying down she sat up.

The two men kept quiet while the predator roared. Kat tried not to sleep. Her eyes kept dropping closed despite wanting to stay awake. She'd jerk and stare at the makeshift blockade.

When light began to creep inside, the animal finally left and Kat finally allowed herself to relax. Curling close to their fire, she vaguely heard the men talking before she fell asleep.

DERRICK

"We need to head back," Robert repeated. "We should have gone back when we found Katie."

"You know why we didn't." Derrick wasn't happy. He enjoyed having her close and not being told, other than by his friend, to stay away from her. She done well despite the cold and made his job much easier.

"Yeah, I know." Robert spared the girl a glance. "You should tell her what we found."

"I can't. Besides, we don't know for sure."

Robert shook his head. "The only way to prove it is to return to the mountain. They can do the tests there."

"You think I don't know that?" he grumped back.

"Today's plan should be," Robert continued as if he were in charge, "pack up the remains. Get a good night's sleep, if that wild hunter out there will let us, and then head back tomorrow morning."

Derrick glared at the other man, not ready to return yet. Not with all the wonderful finds they might make.

"The city is going to be here," Robert reminded him. "We can always come back."

Robert was right even if Derrick didn't want him to be. The only difference was Kat wouldn't be able to come. Their leaders would find a way to keep her in the mountain and make sure she never had a chance to escape again.

Escape? Derrick frowned. The mountain was home. Wasn't it?

As quietly as they could, they ate a bland breakfast of nuts and fruit along with the usual hot drink before going outside. First, they had to move the barricade. Luckily, the sky had cleared although Derrick could see fat clouds slouching over the mountains and heading for the city.

"Think we'll get a storm?"

Robert shaded his eyes. "Maybe. Maybe not. These mountains do strange things to the weather."

True enough. Derrick spent the day helping Robert wrap the remains and place them in the back of their snow cat. All the while he felt like he was being watched so he kept looking around. There didn't seem to be anything.

"What's wrong?"

Derrick shook his head. "Just seems like there should be people here."

"Was once." Robert closed up the vehicle for the night. "Let's get some food and then go to sleep." He grinned. "Don't know about you, but I'm tired."

With a tired smile, Derrick had to agree. They went inside, replaced their barricade and joined Kat, who had made them soup again.

"We're going back to the mountain tomorrow morning," Robert informed her.

Kat scowled. "I don't want to."

"You don't have a choice." Robert ate his soup.

Not really liking how his friend had informed Kat, Derrick ate not talking. He didn't trust what he might say.

As the night fell thick white flakes began to drift down. Cold seeped in and Robert built up the fire.

"Why?" Kat broke the quiet.

"Why what?" Derrick absently asked.

"We have bodies that need to be identified." Robert crawled into his sleeping bag. "We won't know anything until that's done."

Kat bit her lip and Derrick could tell she was trying not to cry.

"Go to bed, Kat." He didn't know what else to say.

She glared at him. He'd never felt so helpless.

CHAPTER 25
WORD WARRIOR

Yowling and growls interrupted my class. "Stay here," I ordered my class as I dashed out into the hall.

At the library door Algier and Mute tumbled over each other. Sasha crouched near the door and behind her lay a kitten. I smelled blood and hissed, my hunches bunching for an attack.

"I'll go for Indrani." I saw the flash of Mitzy's black tail as she ran.

My eyes watched Algier. How dare he! I hissed. Furious. My back legs bunched to attack.

Tomura suddenly darted in front of me. "No, husband. This is Mute's fight. Sasha is his mate."

I knew she was right. My tail swished angrily. I wanted to defend my daughter!

I saw a blur of black. Lara dashed to Sasha's side. Her tongue licked the younger female's muzzle.

Algier and Mute circled, each trying to find a weakness. Sasha's mate had blood dripping down his side. He tripped and Algier pounced.

An angry reroww filled the chilled air. Sheba flew into the fight, her claws tearing at her mate.

Algier fell back, rolled, barely managing to get up. Sheba raked a gash across his nose. Blood dripped down his muzzle onto the dusty floor.

"You are no longer my mate!" she growled.

"I won you in challenge!" he snarled back.

"Any male who would DARE harm a kitten, is no mate I want!"

"She has the right," Starlite said quietly. I hadn't seen her join us. She stood beside me, her fur glistening in the faint light.

"Too much power to females," Algier growled. He cast a disgusted look at Mute. "He didn't deserve Sasha."

"She chose him," Tomura reminded the other male. "You had

no right to challenge."

"The other males are right."

I knew what the other males thought. By choosing to educate their young, the females had begun to decide who to mate with and who not. They'd disrupted the right of challenge by which we had always lived.

"Females always had some rights," Tomura continued. "I could have refused Word Warrior's challenge and stayed with the season's champion." She licked my muzzle. "I chose well."

"You are in the wrong, brother." Starlite took a step forward. He moved back.

"I'm leaving." Algier stepped past Mute who opened his mouth as if to hiss. I saw the older male fight the impulse to attack.

"Where will you go?" Starlite sounded concerned for her brother.

"Most males roam," he replied. "Too noisy around here."

"And who will teach science?" I wanted to know.

"Neutron and Sapphire can." He continued down the hall. I didn't know if we'd ever see him again.

"He'll be back." Starlite watched her brother leave. "He has something he must do."

"And what is that?" I wanted to know what she did.

"When the time is right, you will know." Starlite turned her blue eyes to the injured kitten.

Sasha nosed her kitten, but it wasn't moving. I couldn't even tell if it lived.

A huge white body with black spots brushed past me. I jumped back startled.

Indrani sniffed the youngster and sadly told Sasha, "It is too late."

"I thought so," I heard Sasha reply. "I was hoping Patch would live."

"His neck is broken. Even if he had lived, it would have been more kind to kill him."

Sasha went to Mute. He tried to clean his wound. "Indrani, my mate is hurt."

"I will tend him." She gently took the young male into her mouth and carried him into the library.

Sasha took a final look at Patch before following the Snow Ghost.

"This is the second of us we have lost." Lara blinked.

"First Callie and now Patch." Mitzy sat, her tail trailed behind her.

"Death is part of our life." Starlight glanced once more in the direction her brother had gone. "As is loss."

"You are now without a mate," Tomura said to Sheba.

I was about to invite her to become one of my wives when her next words took me by surprise.

"Mute fought well for his mate. If he will have me, I will be his as well."

"That is your choice?" I didn't know many females who wanted a male who could not hear.

"It will be mine, his and Sasha's." Her tail flipped. "I know he at least will not kill my kittens."

A fatal mistake Algier had made. I could understand his instinct. I'd overcome it myself when I rescued Sasha, yet I had never attacked his or Mute's kittens.

Sheba went into the library and I knew we needed to get back to our classes. First, I had to speak with Neutron.

I found my son already instructing Science. He saw me and paused. "Yes, Word Warrior."

"You now teach Science." I didn't say anything else. There was no need.

"Thank you." He continued teaching.

I returned to my reading class.

As the sun dragged across the sky snow fell. I could barely see outside through the iced window and cold seeped even further into the room. Several of the kittens shivered.

"Word Warrior," Lara stood at the door. "Several mothers came for their kittens and told us the snow is so heavy they barely managed to reach the school."

"There should be enough rats." Food would be important.

"We have to keep the young warm."

"If they snuggle together they should be warm enough."

"Not in the classrooms."

I had to agree. Cold crept even further inside "Is there room for all of us in the library?"

"If we use some of the shelves, perhaps."

"Then start moving them there. Have the mothers help you." She bounced out.

"Come," I instructed my class. "We're going to the library."

"You mean we don't get to go to our mothers?" Bayd protested.

His mother lived the furthest away.

"I don't want you getting lost in the snow. You could freeze. I don't think your mother would like that."

"No," he reluctantly agreed.

I led my class down the hall and into the library. I slowed near the door. Patch's body was gone, but the smell of blood remained. Going past the lingering reminder, we crossed into the library. Mute, Sasha and Sheba were curled together in the nest, Ara and Ice, the surviving kittens almost hidden in Sasha's gray fur. Sheba's much older young were nearby, play fighting with several others.

"Find a warm place," I told my class. "Cuddle together if can't find your litter mates."

"Some could cuddle with me," Indrani volunteered. Her large body flowed around the corner of the faded wood counter. "I have a fine warm spot behind here."

Several from my class floundered over and followed the Spotted Ghost.

"It is good she is here," Tomura said. "I remember many colds, but not like this."

Even I began to feel the cold through my thick fur. "Did Jojo and Nan return to their shelter?" I feared for their safety.

"No. They stayed and have been helping with some of the more advanced readers. They went rat hunting."

Two more warm larger bodies to help keep the kittens warm. More of which scampered into the room. Soon, there were cats everywhere. Some crawled on the shelves and swiped at each other, others curled against their mothers, if they'd managed to arrive, while the rest investigated possible warm spots.

Nan and Jojo entered. Nan had one rat while Jojo carried several in his mouth. They dropped them on the floor and left again.

Hungry kittens devoured the feast, washed themselves as their mothers had taught them and then fell asleep.

After the last had eaten, Nan and Jojo joined us in the library, curling up together and welcoming several cold kittens.

I found a spot with Tomura, several kittens snuggling with us.

The cold deepened as the light faded. I shivered, despite the warmth of my wife and the kittens. Two small bodies moved even closer to me. I licked their heads before closing my eyes.

I did not fall into a deep sleep. Every sound, mewl or creaking roused me.

More than once I opened my eyes to search the room. Feline bodies lay everywhere. The only exception was Jojo. He and Nan slept near the door.

Jojo lifted his muzzle, turning his massive head toward the hallway.

I heard faint familiar clicks on the floor. Lavena and her pack paused at the doorway.

"Word Warrior?" the dominate female woofed.

"Here." I slowly got up. The kittens protested.

"Our den is very cold. May we join you?"

So, the cold had gotten bad for the wolves. "Yes."

The pack entered, carefully moving around kittens. Lavena and her mate found a spot near the shelves. They had just settled when I heard Bayd ask," Can I cuddle with you?"

"Are all the kittens here?" Lavena asked.

"All that were in the school."

"Young are young. Come," she invited Bayd. "I have thick fur."

Crawling next to her, Bayd nestled into her fur. Several other kittens joined him. All over the room, kittens shifted, each trying to find a warmer spot, several moving next to the wolves. I'm glad they had come.

More clicking nails and I listened. Rowena and Dermot appeared carrying their pups by their scruff in their mouths. Iden carried one as well and Cara stood further away. Silently they joined us, settling down with their pups and a few kittens snuggled in as well.

Wind rattled outside, the school shifting restlessly. I settled back down, my head resting on Tomura's back. Faintly she purred, trying to both relax me and the kittens.

Maybe I slept. Maybe I didn't. What I remembered next was a roar such as I had never heard. I wanted to both run and not at the same time. My bones vibrated and I heard the wolves growl.

A large shadow passed by the window. I couldn't clearly see it through the heavy snow.

"Striped One," Indrani snarled. She stood near the end of the counter. I could barely see her white body.

"Dangerous?"

"Extremely. We must protect the young."

The shadow passed by the window again. Claws raked on the

glass hurting my ears.

"It knows we're here." Indrani flowed past the counter to watch the predator from behind a shelf.

"Can it get us?" Bayd asked.

Mewling echoed through the library.

"Be quiet!" I ordered. "Be silent as first-born kittens."

Silence followed my order. More earaches as the scratching continued.

Indrani's tail whipped; her agitation obvious. "I lost a cub to one of these."

"Bad, if take cub." Jojo now stood beside the Snow Ghost.

"Very bad."

Lavena growled.

I don't how long the Striped One paced outside. Eventually it left and we all settled down to sleep, albeit uneasily.

When light began to creep in, it was still very dark. The storm raged. Jojo and Nan fed the kittens rats. Mostly we curled together and slept, keeping each other warm.

CHAPTER 26

KAT

Thick snow drifted down, the heavy clouds overhead dumping their burden on the various buildings. Kat stared out the window, not wanting to wake the two men. Despite it being early morning, it was very dark and extremely cold.

"What the…" Robert growled. He stomped to the window, glaring at the storm.

"I don't think we're going anywhere," Kat informed him, happy they couldn't leave yet. "I can't even see where we're parked."

Derrick joined them, his fingers running over his face. "Blizzard." He glanced at the fire. "Kat, how are our supplies?"

"Low." Leave it to Derrick to be practical.

"Can we last a few days?"

"I think so."

"We should have gone back the mountain," Robert grumbled, before going off into the back. Probably needed to relieve himself, Kat thought.

"Nothing we can do except stay put until the storm passes." Derrick wandered back to the fire pot. Kat followed. "At least our cargo is loaded."

"You aren't going to tell me what you found."

"We don't know anything yet." His expression told her the worst.

"I'll warm water." She set about doing mundane chores just to keep herself busy. Kat didn't want to think about what they might discover once they got back.

Wind slammed against the windows and tore across the roof. She hoped their shelter would stand. "Do you think we'll be okay?"

"Yeah." He took the cup she offered him and sipped his tea.

Robert rejoined them and pulled his sleeping bag around his body. "Best to keep as warm as we can."

Kat couldn't disagree with him. Grabbing her bag, she pulled it around her and moved as close to the fire as she could. Sipping her tea she used it to wash down the nuts and fruit. With any luck, this would be a fast-moving storm and they wouldn't be stuck too long. They wouldn't starve, just be on short rations.

Derrick zipped himself in and sat close to her. Kat tried to ignore him. She couldn't afford to like him too much, despite knowing it was already too late. There wasn't anyone else in the mountain she wanted to be with.

She saw the look Robert sent them. His disapproval made her look down and her cheeks burned. He knew how she felt and would make certain they got separated when they returned. That outcome did not make her happy.

"Where are you apprenticing?" Derrick asked.

"What?" Kat jerked her mind back. "Haven't decided yet. Lin would like me to join her in hydro." She shook her head. "I have a brown thumb. I'm better with animals."

"I'd heard you spend a lot of time at the lake."

"I do. I like feeding the ducks and fish."

"Have to wonder why they put a lake inside a mountain."

"Ever visited the lake?" She drank the last of her tea and set down the cup.

"No." Derrick shivered.

The storm raged outside, the wind rattling the roof and the windows vibrating. She glanced out. All Kat saw was blinding white. "I don't remember such a violent storm."

"Me either." Derrick glanced over at Robert. "At least he's asleep."

Her eyes looked at the older man. He'd settled down and she could see the slow movement of his chest. "Lucky for us."

"Or not," Derrick answered quietly. His cup still rested between his hands. The fire flickered across his handsome face. "You know," he started.

"You don't have to say it." She pulled her bag more tightly around her. Cold crept in despite her best efforts. "I wonder if those animals I saw are okay."

"They've survived for a long time. I don't think you need to worry about them."

"One of the creatures left with me." Kat had no idea why she'd shared that.

"Where is it?"

"I don't know. Found others like it and left."

"Odd." He took another sip.

"Maybe not." She didn't know much about other creatures or their habits. Maybe it made sense for the animal to want to be with another of their kind.

"We can't be together, Kat, no matter how much we want to be. Our leaders will never allow it."

"I know." She shivered. Whether from the cold or the thought of not being with Derrick, she didn't know. "Maybe they're wrong."

She saw Derrick's eyes flick to Robert. "You need to be careful."

"Careful!" her voice rose. "If I were careful, I would never have left the mountain."

"They're going to punish you for it."

"Perhaps I should punish them for all the lies they've told us."

"What lies?" Derrick stared at her.

"When don't they lie?" How could he not see? "We're dying, Derrick, or haven't you noticed?"

"Things have been rough since the fire."

"And getting worse. Lin is worried. She won't say it, but I know the crops are failing. All I had to do was look around hydroponics. The truth is there."

His hand reached out and touched her arm. "You need to be careful. If they exile you,"

She understood the implied threat. "I don't think it would a bad thing. There are other survivors, Derrick."

"We don't know that."

"Don't we?" She had to make him see. "If our leaders thought we were the only ones, they would never have done the computer pings. Never would have," she stopped not wanting to say anything about Mute.

"Far as I know, they didn't get a response."

"You're right." Definitely getting colder and she could feel it creeping up her back. "I just can't believe we were the only ones who made it."

CHAPTER 27

MOON

The elevator ground to a halt and Moon dashed out just ahead of the human feet. They wouldn't deliberately step on her, they were respectful. She jumped up on her favorite perch and watched them disperse. Under her the table wobbled like always. Once tourists had flocked here, now, just the survivors.

The group returning had raided some of the outer most houses where they'd hope to find supplies or even trinkets. They remembered what happened and the past had become more important to them. Not that they had reason to forget. The old records were safe, just as those who had left the treasure behind knew they would be.

Hutchinson, Kansas had once been a small town. The main attractions had been a space museum and the salt mines, where the humans lived. The carved-out caverns had kept them safe through the eruption and the long bitter winter.

She sniffed, noting the scents of dry salt and of humans who bathed infrequently. Water was precious and not wasted. Luckily, Moon didn't need the liquid to keep herself clean. Her tongue did the job quite well.

After the group passed, she jumped down, pausing now and then to gaze into the glass cases. Old books stood open displaying the history of the mine, while others displayed costumes and posters from old movies. Vaguely she remembered places where humans would go to watch them and then view them again at home when they were released.

Odd to think that world had vanished long ago and buried under ash and snow. She remembered the dark cloud raining thick gray, coating the lungs of many who died in those first few hours. Others had managed to escape and come to the mine.

She pushed her mind away from the past. Granted she would retain the details and be able to share them with the kitlings and elders at the next gathering. She'd missed many and would not be at the next. Moon had enjoyed her time on Earth yet she felt the call of home.

Past time since she could have left at any moment when the portal opened. Strange to think when the three moons glowed full in the sky, they created a passage for all her kind to return home to find mates, share their histories and raise kitlings.

Kitlings. Part of her missed the two she'd had on Earth and left in the care of Callie. She'd had no choice at the time and realized much later she should never have left them behind. Moon could only hope they were well and had survived.

Dashing along the dusty floors she jumped aboard one of the traveling machines. The old man driving it chuckled and welcomed her aboard. "Hello, darling."

She blinked and washed her shoulder secretly pleased he always acknowledged her. Some of the humans avoided her and others at least gave her a scratch under her chin or behind her ears. Cats were treasured and fit into community perfectly. They kept the rodent population down and out of the badly needed crops.

Moon played her part although killing mice and rats was not her primary reason for being there. She gathered knowledge and history, which she would share once she traveled home again. As far as she knew, she was the only Felcat who had stayed on Earth after Yellowstone had exploded covering the atmosphere with an ash cloud, cooling temperatures and knocking the planet into an ice age.

"There ya go, darling." The driver stopped.

Her stop. She jumped off and trotted away. Green growing things beckoned and there was a rat she intended to kill for her dinner. He was a wily thing and she'd been after him for weeks. Tonight. Tonight he would die, and she would eat well.

She couldn't wait.

CHAPTER 28
WORD WARRIOR

Two full times of the moon passed before the storm stopped. I don't remember it ever being so cold. We didn't lose any of the kittens or wolf pups. All of us had to work together to keep the young fed and the rats were becoming more difficult to catch. Either there were fewer of them, or they had become more wily.

I stood at the entrance dismayed by the snow pile blocking the way out. Many of the trees had broken and I could not see the underground tunnels we used. I didn't know how long it would take us to get out.

"Not bad." Rowena pushed past me and used her front paws to dig.

I jumped back not wanting to be buried. Snow flew everywhere. She stopped and cocked her large white head.

"More than I thought." She trotted back. "Going to get pack."

To do what I wondered? I followed, passing the empty classrooms and wishing it had been warm enough to continue teaching.

Cold clawed at my fur and I was happy when I reached the library. My wives had claimed a corner and I went to them. "It will take some time before we can leave."

"The storm was bad," Tomura agreed. Her dainty tongue cleaned her fur.

"Worse than I remember."

"All will be well, Word Warrior." Starlight brushed against me.

I felt reassured by her words. If there had been any danger, she would know. Or would she? I sometimes wondered how her gift worked.

"My brother will find his fate." Her blue eyes blinked. "Although not the one he is expecting."

"And ours?"

"Unclear." She sounded sad. "I can see a long journey, but not the outcome."

"Journey?" I asked.

"As I said Word Warrior, my vision is unclear."

The thought of taking a journey chilled me more than the rooms of the school or the expired storm outside. True I had taken many to win my wives and one to bring Callie to us. That had been many moons ago.

"Who takes the journey, Starlite?"

She used her paw to wash her muzzle before she answered. "I see three moons in the sky."

"There's only one," Nan corrected her. "We see it every night."

Jojo stood next to her listening.

"I only know what I see." Starlite rose. "Before that will come a battle." Her eyes surveyed my other wives. "And great loss."

ALGIER

He unfurled his body and proceeded to wash his sandy colored fur with black stripes. Silence surrounded him and despite his wish for it, Algier found he missed he chaotic thoughts he always heard. Kittens wanting to be warm, mothers worrying they may not have enough milk for their young, others planning their school lessons.

Instead his mind found nothing. Lifting his blue eyes to stare out at the vast white before him from the safety he'd found in a small house smelling faintly of an ancient butt sniffer, he was glad the storm had finally stopped. After he'd been kicked out of the school, he headed toward the rising sun. The opposite direction was nothing more than tall mountains he had no desire to cross. Dermot had talked about them endlessly when he'd first come having been born there and living with his pack.

He knew from those tales he would not survive the trek. Too many dangers and even the wolf had not traveled to the other side so Algier had no idea what he might encounter.

Not that he knew what he might encounter by going the other direction. He'd reached the edge of the human houses, most of which had collapsed long ago from the heavy snow and ice. Beyond lay nothing by a vast expanse of white and a tug on him he had to follow. One which he did not understand beyond knowing he must go.

He'd eaten a scrawny rat before the dark fell, but his stomach grumbled. After always having enough, it would be difficult to adjust to only eating when he found prey.

Rising, he stretched his back, feeling relief after spending a couple of suns curled tightly trying to keep warm. He missed Sheba. He snarled remembering she'd rejected him. Now she and their kittens would live with defective Mute, a cat he never understood why Word Warrior allowed to live.

Damp greeted his nose and he gingerly stepped out. The tug yanked on him and he followed it, not knowing where to go only understanding he must.

Part of him dreaded finding out. Part of him couldn't wait to have an adventure.

Moon

She awoke blinking, taking a moment to use her paw to wash her muzzle. Around her the faint murmurings of humans sounded. Some beginning their day, others going to bed since there is no day or night underground. Such did not trouble her. She slept when she wanted. Hunted when she wanted. Allowed humans to pet when she wanted.

A light tug pulled on Moon. Not strong, but enough to let her one of her kitlings journeyed and no doubt searched for her. Still far away. She had no doubt that in time they would meet. She wondered what they looked like full grown. Last time she'd seen them they'd been tiny and weaned.

Moon settled her head back down and observed the humans. Their routines varied little. Those beginning their day went to the cafeteria to eat. Then they would check the documents and old movies stored here to make certain nothing had damaged them. Some would tend the crops, others would go to the surface and scrounge for supplies, if any were truly left. Other times they maintained the elevator, which they had to keep running or else they'd never be able to leave.

Not that they planned to do so now. The storms still raged and she wondered how much longer the winter would last. Not a scientist, yet she knew the great ash cloud covered the planet for many years bringing on the cold.

Her nose detected a slight flowery scent and another cat paused, sitting down and wrapping its black tail over its paws. She was new here. One of the workers brought her down a few days earlier.

That's when the lifeless rodents began showing up. They smelled odd and none of the cats would touch them. The dogs on the other hand, had no problem gobbling up free food.

You do not remember, her thoughts slipped into Moon's mind. *You are not like the other cats either.*

No, she replied. *You are not like me.*

True. She moved her head to watch a human walk by who ignored them. *I have a mission here.*

And what is that?

To protect this place.

Why?

I only know the goddess has requested it. Why are you here?

To study. Learn. Record these events and share them with my people.

The black cat closed her eyes and opened them again. *From where did you come?*

Far away.

Still children of the goddess.

Moon suspected she knew of whom the black cat spoke. On her world, the goddess was but a legend.

With a flick of her tail the other cat bounced away. Moon would learn nothing more today.

Chapter 29

Kat

"Storm's stopped," Robert shared waking Kat.

She poked her head out of sleeping bag. Cold air laced icy fingers into her hair. "So?"

Derrick groaned sitting up, keeping his sleeping bag tightly wrapped around his body. "Your point?"

"Talked to the mountain this morning and they want us back. Now."

"We haven't finished—" Derrick began.

"The bodies need to go back and be identified. They have families waiting."

Kat tried to keep breathing when his words caused her to feel like steel hands griped her ribs. Had they found Ned and not told her? They'd never allowed her to see the bodies.

"Come on, Kat," Derrick urged. "Let's have some food and head back."

"Maybe I don't want to go." Kat would be punished for taking the snow cat.

"Best to face it," Robert told her as if he'd heard her thoughts. "You didn't really think you'd get away with it did you?"

She made a face at him and sat up. Derrick handed her a cup and she sipped the hot contents.

In silence the three shared a breakfast of nuts. They didn't have much else left.

When they finished, they broke camp, loading their camping gear into the machines.

Robert started to get into the one she'd driven, pointing at the passenger door indicating she should get in.

"I'll drive Kat." Derrick glared at the other man.

The two men exchanged looks before Robert shrugged. "Fine. I'll follow you."

Derrick climbed in and she got into the seat next to him.

"What was that all about?" she asked, grabbing her sleeping bag and tucking it around her legs.

"Guy thing," he answered. He started the snow cat and backed up, heading back the direction they'd originally come from. "You know you're in a lot of trouble, right?"

"I just wanted to find out what happened to Ned." She knew the bodies were in the one Robert drove. Her hope of finding her brother alive began fading and she feared the worst.

"Won't matter." He cast her a sympathetic look.

"It should."

"Kat." Derrick sighed. "Don't get your hopes up."

She dared to ask the one question she feared the answer to. "Is Ned's body one of those we're taking back?"

"Don't know." He sighed, rubbing a hand over his chin. "They're too badly damaged."

"Oh." She stared ahead as they crossed some sort of bridge and he turned left, slowly creeping down alongside destroyed buildings on both sides. "I wonder how much warning they had?"

"Enough some of us survived."

"Do you think anyone besides us did?"

"Don't know."

Gray clouds swirled above casting a grim shadow over the landscape. Barren trees reached upward reminding Kat of skeleton fingers. She shivered knowing returning for her would not go well. She'd taken equipment and supplies without permission. Their leaders would not be very happy with her.

The only saving grace was that she was old enough to apprentice and not quite of age for the leaders to select a mate for her. Her eyes darted in Derrick's direction and she blushed. She knew she couldn't be with him, but she so wanted to be.

"Whatever happens," he broke the silence. "Know that I like you and will always be your friend." She saw the sadness in his eyes. "It can never be anything more."

"What they do is wrong," she grouched, trying to slouch in the seat.

"They're only trying to make certain we survive."

"Don't you tire of just surviving?"

"Every day," he breathed. He glanced behind him. "At least with Robert driving the other snow cat, you and I can talk."

"He's been a grouch, huh?"

"Just keeps reminding me of what I should already know."

"Both of us you mean." She pulled the bag further up. Her coat was doing a lousy job of keeping her warm, and she straightened in her seat.

"Want me to turn the heat up?"

She shook her head. "Save the energy. We have a long trip home."

"How's your sister?"

"Busy." She didn't tell him her sister was pretty much sleeping at her job.

"There's a problem isn't there."

Her expression must have given it away. "Might be. Lin doesn't talk about it."

"When our leaders started sending out the teams I suspected something."

"Do they ever tell us the full truth?"

CHAPTER 30

WORD WARRIOR

The pack worked together, managing to clear the entrance so we could leave. Glancing around I almost didn't recognize the school, or the houses surrounding us. I could see roofs sticking above the thick white, a few bare tree branches pointing toward a blue sky. My eyes traveled to the mountains, now covered completely, making them seem like I had never seen them before.

"Bad storm." Jojo stood beside me, Nan at his side.

The other wolves ventured out, lifting their muzzles, releasing howls. They would stop and listen, then begin again.

"They're looking for the other packs," Nan told me.

The ones who had left due to the two-legs whose return they feared. Rowena had shared with me once the two-legs had hunted them until almost none were left. They had reclaimed what was rightfully theirs and had no desire to once again become prey.

Prey. That reminded me of our other problem. The striped one. Not all of the females and their young had reached the safety of the school before the snow came. We would need to discover their fates.

Faint howls answered the pack. I had no doubt Lavena was relieved.

The dominate female howled in answer. A few heartbeats later, a lone howl answered.

Nan brushed against Jojo. "At least they survived."

I felt relief. More who had survived one of the worst storms we'd had for as long as I could remember.

A chill passed through me as if the cold found a way to enter my body. What about the other females who lived in the houses around us? With the wolves howling, I should see them coming across the white to investigate what was going on. Instead nothing moved.

Lavena turned her head toward me, her nose sniffing, her eyes full of worry. "We will go see." She led the pack down the slope, their bodies bouncing as they leaped through the new fallen snow.

"I help." Jojo went in the other direction. He stopped a body length away, turning back to look at Nan.

"You go ahead. It's too deep for me."

He whined.

Dermot dashed out joining the younger male. Together they crossed the large area before going to the nearest house. Three females lived there with their young.

"Do you think they survived?" Nan asked.

"I don't know." I nudged her inside. "Stay with the others. I'm going to check the houses behind the school."

Nan hurried back inside. I watched until I knew she was safe, before carefully trudging through the snow. The easy entrance we usually used was completely blocked and I had to be careful so I would not fall too deep and become buried. Luckily, my large feet kept that from happening.

A lower window stood open and I squeezed inside. Chilled air filled my lungs. Working my way down to the floor, I noticed the icy surface. I climbed several stairs before finding the females. They'd curled together, yet did not rise when I approached them. Their eyes were open, yet I saw no life.

In another room I found blood spattered on the walls and some in the nest. The smell I knew from the attempted attack on the Rowena's cubs. Gazing up, I saw fluttering fabric and below glittering shards. How the striped one had jumped so high and gained access, I had no idea.

Indrani might know and I would speak to her when I returned.

I spent the day searching many houses, finding some dead, others just gone, the stench of predator the only smell I found.

As the sun began to sink behind the mountains, bathing the sky in reds and pinks, I returned to the school. Grimly I listened to the pack's report and to Jojo and Dermot. They had found what I had.

"Found a few young," Jojo shared. "Brought here."

I noticed when I'd returned there seemed to be more. At least some survived the storm and the striped one's hunting.

Indrani listened, along with Jyotis.

"The striped one must be close to having her cubs," Indrani observed. "Once she does, she will hunt again as she must produce milk to feed them."

Putting all of us at risk. I did not like the idea.

"Doesn't she understand we're intelligent?" Nan cocked her head to the side puzzled.

"With the striped ones it makes no difference," Indrani answered. "They hunt all. We are nothing but food for their belly."

"So how do we fight her?" Jyotis flicked her long tail.

The healer fell silent.

I suspected I knew and it was not a solution I would have wished upon any mother.

Her long pink tongue cleaned a spot on her shoulder before Indrani spoke again. "I would be better if we could kill her now, before her cubs are born."

Lavena growled. "Hidden too well."

"She will pick a safe place. One we cannot find."

"The storm covered her scent trail," the male dominate added.

No we wouldn't be able to track the striped in that way. Yet we needed to find the predator and stop her before she killed all of us.

"She will hunt while feeding her cubs," the healer added.

I began to follow where I suspected Indrani led. Much as I hated to kill any innocent cub, I doubted we had a choice.

"We have to kill the cubs." Jyotis had figured it out.

Her brother stood next to her, listening intently.

Lavena blinked. "Bad to kill cubs."

"Very bad," I agreed. "But if we don't, the striped one will kill all of us."

CHAPTER 31

ALGIER

He continued to travel in the direction of the rising sun, across the vast expanse of white. He could see nothing in any direction, yet the pull inside him chose his path. Algier trusted it, although why he wasn't sure.

At least in the expanse of nothing, no other thoughts intruded upon his own. No annoying kittens asking questions about the lesson he had just taught. No females to provide for and no Word Warrior telling him what to do.

How his sister could tolerate the large cat he didn't understand. Starlight adored her mate and the company of his other wives.

What irked him was the deaf cat Mute, who should have been killed, now had his female, plus the only mate Algier had wanted, Sasha. Why she'd chosen such a weak male he didn't understand. Females deserved better.

He stopped, his tale flicking back and forth, strange smells filling his nose. Nothing moved except the wind, catching the snow and twirling it around.

Algeir moved forward. He had no idea how long he would have to travel, but he wanted to know what lay at the end of his journey. No doubt it would be better than what he had left behind.

KAT

Their journey back to the mountain didn't seem to take as long as her first trip to the city. They passed the structure she'd taken shelter in with the posters of animals and continued up the road. She glanced behind to see the other snow cat not far away.

"Didn't trust us to come back on our own did he?" She couldn't help her bitter tone.

"No," Derrick honestly answered. He sighed. "If I'd had my choice…" he stopped as if afraid to voice his thoughts.

Kat sympathized. Conditions in the mountain were only going to get worse just as they had for many years. "We're doomed aren't we?"

He glanced at her uneasily. "Maybe."

They fell silent as the machine plodded upward. Kat feared her return wondering what type of punishment their leaders would find for her. The worst she could picture was an immediate marriage to a man she no desire to be with.

"I contacted someone," she heard herself say.

"What?" His face held shock. "Who?"

"I don't know."

"Did you tell anyone?"

She shook her head, pulling her sleeping bag tighter against her body. The biting cold pierced her skin and she shivered. "I couldn't."

"Why not?" Instead of snapping at her, Derrick sounded more curious.

"I," she paused trying to figure out why she hadn't. "I liked having a secret." Kat moved her legs, trying to warm them. Part of her was terrified someone else may have found the messages and her responses.

"Keeping a secret of such importance could get you into a lot more trouble." Derrick puffed out air. "Did they tell you anything?"

"No." Kat frowned. "Their answers were strange and I didn't understand them."

"Strange how?"

"Almost like they weren't human." She bit her lip. "That's not possible is it?"

A silence followed her question. Her eyes took in the bleak white and skeleton trees. Any sign of her earlier travels had been covered by the last storm.

"Look, Kat," Derrick began, "if by chance one of those bodies is your brother's," he stopped.

"If it is," she quietly replied, "at least I'll know what happened to him."

"We found animal bodies too."

"You did?" She focused her attention on him.

"Yeah. Didn't make sense."

"They didn't?" she was afraid to ask.

"We won't know the entire stories until the remains have been identified and autopsied."

A shudder ran through her body. She knew what he meant and she hated the idea of someone cutting up her brother's body to find out why he died.

"I'll be here for you." His determined look told Kat more than words ever would.

SHADOW

She'd promised the goddess she'd protect and look after the human records. Not a difficult assignment, since the protectors of knowledge worked diligently to preserve the history of humanity before the eruption and the long winter.

A spot itched one her shoulder and she cleaned it. The rat she'd killed had bit her before it died. Not that she'd suffer any harm from it. A normal cat would have, but she was a Chosen One. Its blood had been satisfying just as the battle had been.

Her yellow eyes blinked as she settled down in a dark corner, her intent to take a nap. Since it was normally dark in the mines, she had no reason to seek out a safe hiding place to pass the day.

In the distance voices rose and fell, and she listened to sounds which had become familiar, the thumping of the water pump, the screech of the elevator as it rose to the surface and the thud when it returned again, along with the scratching of pages as the boxes were sorted.

As her eyes closed, her memory replayed images of days long gone.

The eruption of a volcano smothering the sun, land, humans and animals. Some survived by hiding like rabbits or prairie dogs in prepared places. Others perished in their homes or choked while trying to flee or worse, got caught in a fast-moving gray cloud.

A story she'd heard once from another Chosen one about a child who they'd comforted as the bitter cold claimed them, while a harsh tale, also a treasured one.

Rumors of the last colony ship that had managed to escape just as volcano ripped open spewing gasses and suffocating clouds. She wondered what had become of those who had traveled in it.

Sleep finally claimed her, and she wondered how long Bast meant for her to stay.

CHAPTER 32

KAT

"Your actions were irresponsible," one of their leaders shouted at her. "You put everyone in danger!"

An older man dressed in thick coats, sitting across the metal table from her, leaned forward. "What do you have to say for yourself?"

Kat pulled her coat tighter around her. As soon as she'd returned, Lin had met her with a stern and worried look. "It's bad," she whispered, as she gave Kat a hug.

Robert had glared at the reunion, before marching away. Kat had been sure he was going to make his report to the leaders.

"You'll only have a few minutes." Lin walked with her toward the main conference room. Some of the walls had ice forming on them and icicles hung along the ceiling.

"How bad, Lin?"

"Bad." Her sister hadn't had time to tell her more before she'd been whisked inside by Robert who grabbed her arm.

His smirk did not give her a great deal of confidence. Derrick sat at the table, his voice giving the details of their mission. They'd lost two because of a polar bear attack but had managed to recover the bodies of the missing missions.

"We'll get to work on them," a female leader assured them all.

When Derrick finished his report, he'd given her a sympathetic look and left. Robert ignored her, giving the leaders a nod as he closed the door.

Hours later after sharing all she'd seen and learned the leaders had begun what she knew was coming.

"I'm sorry. I wanted to find my brother." Her heart beat faster and she feared the worst.

The old one tapped his fingers on the table. "You may have. We should have the autopsy in a few hours."

"What if we had needed the snow cat?" The man who had

yelled at her earlier glared, making her want to hide under the table.

She glanced down dull surface, resisting the urge to draw designs with her fingers. "I didn't think about that."

"You should have," he growled at her.

"Enough," the old one interceded. "I'm sure Kat has learned her lesson and it will not happen again." He sat back. "We have parties who have returned and the rest will be here soon."

His comment was news to her and she wondered if during her absence they'd reported in.

His attention re-focused on her. "One of the cats went missing. Do you know anything about it?"

She'd forgotten about the cat. "It rode with me into the city and then left. I have no idea where it went."

"The animals you saw." The woman gazed intently at her. She'd been silent up to now, her gray hair wrapped around her head. "Tell us about them."

"They were cats and a wolf." She shrugged. "Nothing remarkable about them."

The group exchanged meaningful looks.

"Are you certain?" she pressed. Her frame seemed swallowed in her green clothes.

"They were just walking away." Why they wanted to know puzzled Kat. What could be so important about a bunch of animals?

"Did they do anything strange?"

"No." Not that she'd noticed anyway.

"But her actions," the man began again.

"Enough," the oldest interrupted. "Although I can't condone what she did, her travels have given us more information."

The woman nodded. "Agreed. You'll resume your duties in the com room tonight. I suggest eating and taking a nap."

"Yes, ma'am." Kat rose, grateful she hadn't received punishment for her actions.

The old man spoke again, "This time only, will your actions be overlooked. Should there be a repeat offense, you will not fair as lightly."

"I understand. Thank you." Kat hurried from the room before they changed their minds.

Lin waited for her. "Well?"

"I made a report and was told not to make the same mistake

again."

"Nothing else?"

Kat shook her head.

"Huh." Lin glanced at the closed door. "That doesn't bode well."

"I don't' care." She didn't. "I'm just thankful since I know it could have been worse."

"A lot worse," Lin agreed. "I'm hungry."

Kat's stomach growled. She couldn't remember when she'd eaten last. "Me too."

They hurried down the darkened corridor toward the cafeteria. Mixed smells of pasta, cheese, and spices greeted them as well as warmth.

"About the only room that never gets cold," Lin told her softly, glancing around to make certain she hadn't been overheard.

"What is going on here?" Kat noticed how everyone in the room sat in small groups, hunch together, casting uneasy glances about the room.

"Let's get some food first."

After filling their plates and grabbing some tea, they found an empty table near the back. Kat sipped her lukewarm beverage and made a face.

"Yeah," Lin agreed. She ate a slice of orange. "More systems collapsed while you were gone."

"Like the heat."

"Yes." Lin sipped her tea. "The leaders won't admit it, but rumors say we might have to abandon the mountain."

"And go where?" Kat shook her head. "There's nothing but cold and snow everywhere."

"I have no idea." Lin lowered her voice even more. "From what I heard they pinged the computers again."

Kat swallowed hard. Had they found out she'd been talking to someone one in the city? "And?"

"There might have been an answer or two. I don't know the details."

Kat really hoped they hadn't found out she'd been talking to anyone. If they had, it might go very badly for her since she hadn't reported the incident. "They asked me about the animals I saw. Any idea why?"

Lin shook her head. "No."

Taking her sister at her word, Kat changed the subject and they talked about other family stuff, mostly memories about their brother. While she hoped his wasn't one of the bodies Derrick and Robert had found, she had a sinking feeling in her stomach that he was.

NAN

Nan sat outside the school. Jojo played with Rowena's pups while she and her mate Dermot hunted. They'd gone a few sunsets without the striped one prowling and threatening them. She'd overheard Indrani saying she thought perhaps the large feline had finally had her cubs and may not be hunting far from whatever den had been chosen.

Briefly she wondered what the cubs looked like before she pushed her curiosity away. No need to speculate on an event she would not witness.

Jojo chased the cubs toward her and they stumbled around her, barking and wagging their tails. Her mate came to sit beside her and she felt warmer.

One of the cubs nipped Jojo's tail and he chased the young cub. The others floundered after them, often disappearing into the snow.

"Always good to see the young playing," Indrani said as she joined Nan. "Do you and Jojo intend to return to your chosen den?"

"No." They'd discussed it during the last storm. "With not knowing were the striped one is, we think it would be better if we stayed closed and helped protect the school."

"No doubt," the snow ghost agreed. Her pink tongue cleaned her spotted shoulder, her long tail tucked over large paws.

"Does Word Warrior truly intend to search for the striped one's den?" She'd overheard him discussing it with his females after the last sunset.

"Lavena and her pack will help him." Indrani blinked. "We must discover where the striped one is so we do not lose anymore females or their young."

Nan understood. Many of the females and their kittens had died during the last snowstorm. Not from being cold, but because they had become food. "I don't understand why we can't be friends."

"The striped ones have long hunted all others. They stand alone, unlike us."

"I'm going too." Jyotis joined them, his long tail swaying slowly.

Indrani turned her head toward the male. "You are certain you wish to scent this trail?"

"The striped one threatens all of us." His head turned, his eyes following Jojo and Rowena's cubs. "I am not afraid to hunt."

"You need to be taught." Indrani rose.

"You have taught me to find my food."

"But not to fight. Come." She trotted down the incline. Valmiki bounced after her.

Nan didn't want to know what the healer would teach him.

MUTE

His friend had not communicated after many sunsets and rises. Mute stared at the screen, wishing a new message would appear. He wondered if the other had become prey.

About to turn it off, he stopped when a new message flashed. Excited, he pressed the button to read more.

HI MUTE. SORRY I HAVEN'T SENT A MESSAGE IN A LONG TIME. I WENT ON A JOURNEY TO THE CITY.

He sent back. YOU WERE IN THE CITY?

A few heartbeats passed before his friend responded. I WAS. WITH OTHERS LIKE ME. THEY MADE ME COME HOME.

YOU SHOULD HAVE COME TO THE SCHOOL. WE WOULD HAVE HELPED YOU.

SCHOOL? HOW COULD YOU POSSIBLY SURVIVE IN A SCHOOL?

WE HAVE WAYS TO KEEP WARM AND FEED OURSELVES.

RATS! UGH.

THEY ARE EVERYWHERE AND WE HUNT THEM.

HUNT THEM? WHAT ABOUT VEGETABLES AND FRUIT. DON'T YOU HAVE ANY OF THOSE? CAN'T YOU GROW THEM?

WE HAVE ALWAYS EATEN RATS.

WHY?

BECAUSE THEY ARE PREY.

PREY?

OF COURSE. SURELY YOU HUNT AND EAT PREY.

He blinked and wondered if his friend would reply. Surely they understood rats were how they survived.

MUTE, I HAVE A VERY IMPORTANT QUESTION TO ASK AND I

KNOW IT MAY SOUND SILLY, BUT YOU'RE HUMAN? RIGHT?

WE KNOW ABOUT HUMANS FROM THE BOOKS WE READ. WE'VE SEEN TWO-LEGS COME AND GO. THE WOLVES FEAR THEM.

WOLVES?

THE WOLVES JOINED US MANY SUNSETS AGO AS DID THE SNOW GHOSTS.

WHAT ARE SNOW GHOSTS?

LARGE CATS, WHITE WITH SPOTS. THEY'RE LIKE US IN MANY WAYS.

WAIT, LIKE YOU?

Mute tipped his head, wondering why the other was surprised. OF COURSE.

MUTE, ARE YOU...A...CAT?

THAT'S WHAT THE HUMANS ONCE CALLED US.

I'M TALKING TO A CAT?

Puzzled, Mute debated whether or not he should answer. When no more messages appeared, he shut down the computer and went hunting.

CHAPTER 33

KAT

"Who are you talking to?" Derrick demanded.

Kat jumped and whirled in her seat, glaring at Derrick. She hadn't heard him behind her. "My friend Mute. He lives in the city."

"Is that who you went searching for?"

"No!" She rose, a shiver running through her. Whether from fear or cold she couldn't be sure. "I went looking for my brother."

Derrick glanced at the screen, reading the conversation. "You're talking to a…" His face held disbelief. "A cat?"

She sighed. "I thought it was another survivor."

"Do you have any idea how our leaders will react if they discover that."

"That what?" They both turned to find Robert standing inside the com room. "What discovery did you make Kat that you failed to share?"

She moved to shut off the computer. Robert's hand grabbed her wrist and shoved her away, causing her to almost fall. Derrick caught her before she hit the cold hard floor.

"You hurt me!" she yelled at him.

"I'm going to do a lot more."

Derrick moved to stop Robert.

The older man glared at them both. "Don't move."

"Get away from the computer, Robert." Derrick stepped in front of her.

"Derrick don't," she pleaded. "It doesn't matter." Kat couldn't believe she'd been talking to a cat. They weren't intelligent. They couldn't be.

"You've been talking to this…creature for a long time." Robert must have had time to skim the record. He gave her a hard look. "Did you have any idea what it was?"

"I don't believe it's a cat. That's ridiculous!" She rubbed her wrist.

Robert narrowed his eyes. "Have you spent any time with the

animals our earlier expeditions brought back?"

"Not really." Other than the cat she'd traveled with. Kat had no intention of sharing that piece of information.

"They aren't normal." His eyes traveled back to the screen. "If they could learn to run a computer, what else are they capable of doing?" Did she hear a hint of fear in his voice?

"I'm sure Mute is just playing a trick." She hoped so. Her mind couldn't fathom it being anything else.

"Our leaders need to know about this." Robert strode toward the door.

Derrick launched himself at the other man and knocked him to the floor. They rolled around, punching at each other.

Kat moved away, not wanting to become part of their fight.

"You young idiot," Robert growled as they grappled on the floor. "We're in danger. Can't you see that?"

"No." She watched Derrick try to pin the other.

Robert managed to toss Derrick off him. "The wolves." He wiped a bit of blood off his lip. "They killed our scouting party."

"What?" Derrick stared at him. "But we found a cub's body. Maybe, they were just defending themselves."

Robert looked directly at her. "Wolves killed your brother. Think about it, Kat. You may be talking to the enemy."

"How do you know?" she demanded, not willing to believe what he'd just told her.

"Our leaders haven't officially released the autopsy results yet. When they do, we're going to hunt down those animals and kill them."

"For defending themselves?" She couldn't believe what he'd said. "How does that make us any better?"

"They're animals!" He pointed at the computer. "You'd better hope your friend is telling a joke because if we learn those...creatures...have become intelligent, we're going to hunt down and destroy every one of them."

"Why?" She couldn't understand why anyone would do that.

"Because we intend to reclaim what is rightfully ours."

"It's theirs too," she reminded him.

He snorted. "No." Robert turned to walk away.

She covered her mouth to keep from shouting a warning. Derrick picked up a chair and broke it over Robert's back. He fell and didn't move.

"Did you kill him?" Kat hated her voice trembled.

Derrick knelt beside the other main and checked his neck for a pulse. "No. He's still alive." He rose. "Kat, delete every message you got from Mute and send one last one. Tell him if he's really a cat, to run. They need to leave the city."

"You don't really think our leaders would slaughter animals just because they're intelligent."

Derrick's face held a look she'd never seen before. "They would."

Word Warrior

We searched another house and found blood, but no feline bodies. A doorway in the back of the dwelling had been smashed in and long claw marks left on the walls. My nose detected the same strong urine scent we'd found in other places we'd searched.

"Trying to mark her place," Jojo snarled.

Nan stood beside the young wolf. "Stinks."

I agreed with my daughter. The bitter stench of blood and striped one had made the house repulsive. With sadness I left, the pair following. More gone. How many others had been killed?

Glancing across the snow I wondered if Indrani and Valmiki found more of what we had. When we gathered before the dark, we would know.

The three of us walked over the glittering snow headed back to the school. My wives and kittens had resettled there along with any survivors we had found. I wondered if having all of us in the same spot would protect us or place us all in danger.

When we reached the entrance Sasha waited for us. "Mute got a message you need to see."

She led the way down the cold hallway and we entered the library. Most of the cats had settled in the large room, lounging on shelves or claiming spots as their own. Mothers bathed or fed their young. Others played games of chase or pounced on each other.

I jumped up on the counter where Mute sat next to the computer. He turned his eyes to me and pointed this nose as he edged back so I could look at the message.

MUTE. SOMEONE VERY DANGEROUS HAS SEEN OUR MESSAGES.

HE'S GOING TO TELL OUR LEADERS. WHILE WE CAN'T BE SURE, FROM WHAT WE KNOW OF THEM, THEY'LL COME AFTER YOU AND KILL EVERY CAT, WOLF, AND SNOW GHOST.

YOU NEED TO LEAVE THE CITY FOR YOUR OWN PROTECTION.

"As I said husband," Starlight stood beside me. I had not sensed when she joined me. "We will be going on a journey."

"There's nowhere for us to go."

Her blue eyes blinked at me, before looking out as if she saw what I could not. "There is a place, but it will take time to reach."

"Where?" I demanded.

"Far away." Her tail swayed. "Others similar to us and yet different, will delight in our arrival."

I knew she saw things I couldn't, but the vagueness of her words troubled me. More details would have helped. "Will it be a good place?"

"It will." Her gaze passed over my wives. "Not all of us will be going."

I couldn't imagine my wives not being with me. They would go wherever I did. They already had.

"Don't share this message with anyone," I warned Starlight.

She licked my muzzle and jumped down.

"Sasha," I addressed the cat I had spared as a kitten. "Tell Mute to destroy all the messages. If the humans come here, I want them to find nothing." While I had not been aware of the messages he'd sent or the responses, I was grateful we'd been warned of a new danger.

"I'll tell him," she promised.

Indrani appeared in the doorway. "Word Warrior, you must come."

I joined her and we gathered in a room. Rowena and Dermot, along with Lavena and her mate, Valmiki and Indrani.

"We found the striped one's den," Indrani informed us.

Valmiki continued, "We could hear the cubs."

So she'd had her young. I knew her hunting would be more fierce and dangerous for us.

"There is a place close and yet far enough away the female did not think we would find them."

"It's a large place, "Valmiki added. "Full of old human things."

Dermot growled. "The striped one tried to kill our cubs."

Uneasy, I listened, not sure what decision we should make. True the female had killed many of us, and part of me wanted to take her life. Another part feared what might happen if we failed.

"We have the right." Lavina sat, her large body bumping her mate's.

The dominate female was correct. We did. But did we have the right to kill her cubs?

CHAPTER 34

SITA

Her cubs nestled against her, taking her milk, while her tongue cleaned them. They were growing quickly and the time would come soon when she would teach them what they could hunt and devour. After all, every life they took belonged to them.

Outside bright light faded into her favorite time. Dark covered her and she could hunt without being seen.

Close by several of the howlers had made a den. Cubs had been added and they were easier to catch than the grown ones. Unless of course, they'd been injured and then they were easy prey. She'd eaten many.

One of her cubs cried out and she quickly soothed the young male. He was smaller than the others and she doubted he'd survive. Wouldn't be the first she'd lost.

Resting her head on her large paws, she allowed herself a brief sleep. She'd rise later, after making certain her cubs would be warm enough and hunt.

The small felines who proved good snacks, but not a filling meal, would not be what she hunted. Instead, she'd wait near the howlers, hoping they'd either leave their den or one would go off alone.

She might have to wait until after the light came. If successful, Sita would eat well.

INDRANI

"I will have no part of it," Indrani objected. "I will kill the striped one, but not her cubs."

"It makes no difference," Rowena pointed out. "Kill the mother and the cubs will die."

"Killing them would be better. They won't suffer," Dermot agreed.

Word Warrior had been listening, yet not saying much. Indrani wondered what he thought.

"All of us are in danger." The feline leader cleaned a spot on his striped shoulder. "We need to think about this before we hunt and kill."

Valmiki hissed. She worried about what he thought.

"My pack will guard this night," Lavena offered. "The striped one will not find us asleep or easy prey."

Her mate rose and left, his nails clicking on the floor. No doubt he would rouse the pack.

"Then we agree not to attack the striped one until we are certain we can win." Word Warrior spoke as if to make sure they all would wait.

"For now." Rowena and Dermot trotted away. No doubt time for their cubs to drink their mother's milk.

Indrani chuffed her agreement and watched Word Warrior leave.

"He's wrong." Valmiki turned his head toward her. "You were threatened many times by the striped ones. You know."

"We have to all agree," she reminded the young male.

"Do we?"

VALMIKI

Several times the sun rose in the sky. All who searched for the missing told of more dead females and their kittens. Those who survived had moved into the school for safety and the wolves patrolled the entrances, waiting to see if the striped one would dare to attack. They snarled at every moving shadow, their teeth bared, ready for battle.

Valmiki understood how the pack felt. He too wanted nothing more than to sink his fangs into the neck of the striped one, until the female no longer could breathe and died, her blood dripping onto his tongue.

Restless and tired of watching kittens play, females grooming or feeding them, he trotted down the hall and out the front door. Lavena watched him go, a faint yip following him.

Down the incline and across the crusted snow he traveled, light snow falling upon his white, black spotted fur. The storm's scent told him it would not be heavy. Above the stars were hidden from his view. He wondered how Algier fared and hoped the male had not fallen prey to any predator.

He moved past the abandoned human dwellings and behind the large place where he, Indrani and his sister Jyotis had denned. Heavy snow had caused more walls to collapse, and it hung like a rat would from his mouth.

Past other large dwellings whose purpose he did not understand, he sniffed the ground and wrinkled his nose. Claimed territory of the striped one and he dared to trespass, keeping as hidden as he could behind broken walls. Silently his feet moved forward, coming closer to the predator's den.

The large, damaged building stood high above the snow. He entered, his eyes taking in the open dead places. Very little remained except things he did not understand.

Several devices with buttons and empty drawers stood open and he cocked his head. No smell of those lingered.

Padding through the place, he entered the very dark part. Doors hung on their hinges, splintered into many pieces.

No sounds reached his ears and he hoped the striped one had not moved her cubs.

CHAPTER 35

KAT

"How could you keep such a secret?" Lin demanded, anger burning in her eyes. "Our leaders will be furious with you."

"That's why we can't tell them." Derrick paced the small warm room and Kat watched him.

"Can you imagine how they would react if they found out I'd been talking to cat?" She hoped her sister understood.

"How's Robert?" Lin turned her attention to Derrick. Kat didn't know whether to be relieved or angry.

"Still unconscious." He rubbed the back of his neck. "With any luck he'll stay that way until we figure out what to do."

"Do you think he'll remember?" If he did, Kat was terrified of what he'd do.

"No idea."

Lin glanced out at the plants. Kat could tell more had died.

"How long do we have?" Derrick asked her sister.

"Not as long as I'd hoped." Lin sat on the bed, putting her face in her hands. Kat sat beside her, giving her a half hug trying to be reassuring.

Derrick shook his head. "Surely they see we can't continue to stay here."

Lin rubbed her eyes. Kat could see she was exhausted. "They see no such thing. I heard rumors they're going to ration what food we have."

With a frown, Derrick took another look at the plants. "That isn't going to solve anything."

"They're not looking for solutions." Lin sighed.

"If they think the animals are competition, they'll do all they can to destroy them." Derrick sounded angry.

"Which is ridiculous," Kat added. "They have as much right to be here as we do."

"You heard Robert."

"I did yes. Surely our leaders wouldn't do such a thing."

Lin rose. "I think they would." She closed the door so the technician who had just entered wouldn't hear them. "They've been watching many of the animals our teams brought back."

"So?" Kat shrugged.

"So, many don't act the way our remaining videos and books show. The wolves fight being trained and the cats watch us like we're they're studying us." Lin shivered. "It's unnerving."

Derrick and Kat exchanged a look. They hadn't told Lin about the warning they'd sent Mute.

"Maybe with conditions so harsh, they had to evolve in order to survive." Kat hoped Lin would grasp Derrick's meaning.

"Maybe," she agreed. "But we've always been taught when the land is ready again, it is ours to claim."

VALMIKI

Sniffing, slicking low and stalking, Valmiki found the cubs. Their mother had only moved them a short distance and tucked them under a low hanging object. He rested on his belly staring at them. One was white and the other two orange. Their little paws twitched as they slept, the three wrapped around each other for warmth.

Part of him regretted what he had to do. Another knew he had no other choice. They could not be allowed to grow to full size. He had no doubt they'd be taught to hunt the cats, wolves, Indrani, his sister and him.

He listened to the quiet. No doubt their mother hunted. Now was the perfect time. Quickly he struck, killing each quickly, the cubs never waking or even aware of their danger.

When they died, he jumped to a high perch. Now all he had to do was wait.

WORD WARRIOR

The striped one's roar felt as if it clawed past my fur, my body and into my bones. I hissed, my tail whipping, a faint dust cloud following.

Every cat in the library had fallen silent. Rowena quieted her cubs who had whined. Indrani and Jyotis stood in the library door, as if waiting for the striped one to attack.

We heard the large feline prowl past, snarling.

When nothing happened, I knew I could not relax. Danger circled our home.

"Leave it be husband." Tomura stood beside me, her warm sleek body brushing mine. "That one hunts only and I suspect is frustrated we have found a way to escape her."

"For tonight." Starlite glanced out the window. "She will return."

"She's gotten used to easy prey." Indrani joined us. "This night she will find it more difficult."

"As it was at times for us." Jyotis flicked her long tail. "Where did Valmiki go?"

Starlight stared out the door. "To do what we could not."

"Surely not." Indrani stared at my wife.

"No good will come of it. We will need to be ready."

Dread filled me at her words.

SHADOW

She glanced over the boxes filled with documents. Most of these were not important. They belonged to those long dead, buried under the ash and then the snow. Behind her were long metal shelves filled with movies and books. Those were important. A legacy left behind for those of future generations to share.

Bast had not told her exactly what would come. Only there were those who respected nothing and would seek to destroy all which told of the human past. Why they would wish to do this, she did not truly understand.

Would not be the first time.

Shadow turned her head, blinking yellow eyes at the other cat who was different.

We know much of Earth's past. The white cat sat, watching me. Her fur almost seemed to glisten, even in the pale light.

Yet you do not share.

Only when the time of the three moons arrives.

Earth only has one.

Where I come from there are three.

~ 151 ~

Shadow didn't understand. She knew only of one world. The one on which she walked and had been one of the few females to be selected as a Chosen One.

You are aptly called.

I serve Bast.

As well you should.

The other stretched her body. *I will leave you to your musings.* She licked a spot on her shoulder. *Know this Shadow, a time will come when you have a choice. Make it wisely.*

She watched as the other left, confused by the other's words, yet sensing some deep truth unknown to her.

VALMIKI

The striped one appeared and he watched her. He heard her growl of fury and her frantic attempts to rouse cubs long dead. Valmiki wished he felt some triumphant in his victory, yet a sadness filled him. Her suffering was not too different from how he'd felt when his mother disappeared and the wolf found them to bring them to Word Warrior.

Valmiki had no idea by whose claw his mother had died. If he had, perhaps he would have tracked them. Except he'd been too young then and many storms would have covered her tracks and scent.

The striped one yowled again, her head underneath. She would not see him.

Valmiki jumped on her back, his claws raking along into her skin.

She jumped, hitting her head, before managing to back out. With a snarl, she shook him off and pounced, trying to catch his throat in her mouth.

He backed away, hissing, watching her every movement. It would be the only warning he had.

Her large paw swiped at him and missed.

"I killed them," he told her, doubtful she'd understand. None had ever spoken to the striped ones before. "You and they are dangerous and you've eaten too many of us."

Her body tensed and he readied himself. With a leap she was on him and they rolled across the cold, hard floor. They tore at each other with their teeth. Her blood and skin filled his mouth.

They broke apart, each circling the other. Warm liquid trickled down his back and onto his paws. His sides heaved and it was difficult to breathe.

She growled and he felt it penetrate deep, before she grabbed his throat and held on. As his life slowly left him, he saw Sekhmet standing near, ready to receive him.

SITA

This one had killed her cubs, so his life rightfully belonged to her. No doubt he'd come because none of the others had the courage to fight her. She admired him for that, even as she tore his flesh and ate him. He'd fill her empty belly.

She would require rest and several sleeps to regain her strength. When she was strong again, she would go back to where they all cowered. They were her rightful prey and she intended to claim every single one of them.

CHAPTER 36

STARLIGHT

She awoke from a dream filled with violence, blood and death. Starlite knew a horrible fight had occurred, followed by death, setting into motion events that would determine the future of every cat, wolf and Snow Ghost.

Raising her head from Mitzy's back, she looked over the others she shared this nest with. In her heart she knew many would not survive the coming battle and it saddened her.

"Valmiki is dead."

Starlite gazed at Indrani. "He is."

"Foolish." The healer sat her long tail behind her.

Not far away Jyotis slept, several kittens snuggled against her.

"Much is about to change." Again the image of three moons pressed themselves upon her, their meaning unclear.

"Already has." Indrani seemed sad. "I will tell Jyotis when she wakes."

"I will tell Word Warrior and the others. We will need to be ready."

Indrani made no reply. The snow ghost padded away.

Nan and Jojo entered, curling up together. Odd to think they were mated. Not like Starlite was with Word Warrior. The pair would never have young.

She closed her eyes and dreamed again.

WORD WARRIOR

"Father!" Nan called as she hurried down the hall toward the library.

I heard her cry and went to the door. She stopped, blinking her eyes before speaking. "Father, there's something," she paused as if unsure how to continue, "outside...I need to show you."

Light had barely crept through the windows as I hurried after her. Where had Nan gone alone? Jojo rarely left her side. Where was her mate?

Outside cold claws tried to rake through my thick fur. The smell of blood reached my nose and I hissed.

Lying just outside the door I saw the ripped white fur with black spots. It had not been there when the sun set behind the mountains. Starlight had told me Valmiki was dead. I had hoped he'd gone on a distance hunt and her dream would not be true.

Jojo edged around the brick corner, his nose searching in the snow. "Striped one," he informed me. "Here. Not long ago."

My tail whipped back and forth as fury grew in me. How dare the female bring only a piece of Valmiki back to us!

Indrani stepped around me, sniffing the partial carcass. She snarled and backed away. "She ate him."

"Ate him?" Nan asked horror in her tone.

"Ate him," the healer confirmed. "This is a challenge, Word Warrior. The striped one's method of telling us this is her territory, and she will devour all who live here."

"Father?" Nan's yellow eyes met mine. "What are we going to do?"

"You're sure it's a challenge?" I needed confirmation from Indrani.

"A clear challenge," Indrani confirmed. "She knows where we are and dared to bring back Valmiki's remains for us to find."

"Now do what?" Jojo stood protectively beside my daughter. "Bad stink pee along building."

Marking the striped one's territory and letting us know she considered our building hers. We'd been here for many moons and made this place ours. A safe haven for females and their kittens. A place for their young to learn. A new beginning for all cats. The striped one threatened all we'd accomplished and would no doubt eat every one. *If* we allowed the female to live.

"She cannot live, Word Warrior," Lavena joined us. "The striped one must die."

I agreed, yet knew the danger I would place all who resided in the school in. We must have a plan. A strong one to defeat the danger seeking to destroy us all.

"Few have survived a battle with a striped one." Indrani glanced back at Valmiki's fur. "I had no idea he planned to battle alone."

"Cubs alive?" Jojo wanted to know.

"I am not certain." Indrani slowly closed her yellow eyes and opened them. "Difficult to know how the striped one would react whether he merely threatened them or killed."

"Placed us in danger," I interjected.

"He may have tried to kill the mother on his own." Indrani sniffed the fur again. "Her scent is there."

"Not just from having brought this to us?" I had to be sure.

"There are other smells too. He was close to the cubs."

I had to assume he'd killed them and now the striped one would take vengeance on us all. Every cat, kitten, wolf, cub and snow ghost.

Indrani knew the enemy who stalked us better than any other. Her expertise could mean the difference between life and death.

"What do you suggest?" I waited for her answer.

"If we move, she will track us. If we stay, she will hunt until we are all eaten."

No matter what decision I made, we would lose. We needed another way out of the school if the striped one attacked. A way she could not find us. The cats could use the underground pipes, but not the wolves or the snow ghosts. They were too large.

"Not a decision you need make alone," Indrani reminded me. "Often we have solved what seemed impossible together. So should we again."

Call a meeting of all. "Lavena, would the other packs come to our aid?"

"No. They made their decision already."

We'd have no reinforcements. Only those of us still at the school would be there to face the large feline.

"We will watch the door," Lavena promised.

"Watch," I agreed, "but do not attack."

The wolf dominate growled. She didn't like not being able to fight an enemy. I understood how she felt.

"We have too many young who need to be protected." I had to remind her what we protected.

"We are not prey."

"We are not." I agreed. "We will fight. On our terms."

"Good." Lavena turned to her mate and the two of them took up positions by the door. "We will watch."

"Jojo and I will watch during the dark." Nan looked at her mate.

"Jyotis will join you." Indrani stared at Valmiki's fur. "I will tell her about her brother." The healer returned inside. Nan and Jojo followed.

I stared out over the hill where we'd lived for so long. A feeling of loss filled me. Yet, Starlite had told me we would journey, although not all of us. She would not say who not be there, but I feared the worse. Not just myself, my wives and kittens, but all who had trusted me to lead them.

SITA

The plan to leave the ghost's fur had been impulsive. She wanted them to know what would happen to them and how they would all die, just as her cubs had. Painfully, slowly, ripped apart by her claws and fangs, meat to fill her belly.

She curled into her nest. Her cubs' bodies were gone already. They'd been meat. No other choice could have been made. Her actions protected their bodies from scavengers.

Closing her eyes, she knew she would soon return, kill them all, and fill her belly.

CHAPTER 37

KAT

"Come quick," Derrick urged. He breathed quickly and she wondered why.

"What?" Kat had been listening for other teams to report in and Derrick's interruption hadn't been expected.

"Come quick," he repeated, tugging at her arm.

"You know they'll punish me for abandoning my post."

"None of the other teams are going to report in." He paused, swallowed, before continuing. "They can't."

"What do you mean they can't?" She refused to allow Derrick, no matter how much she liked him, to get her into any more trouble.

He took a deep breath. "I overheard our leaders. Most of the teams are dead or stranded and won't risk trying to walk back. They wouldn't survive."

"How do they know?"

"Olga's good at keeping secrets."

Kat blinked. "Olga knew and didn't say anything?" She shouldn't have been surprised. Not really.

"Yes." He tugged her arm again. "Come on."

Knowing full well how much trouble she could get into, Kat rose and followed him out of the com room. Cold hit her body and she shivered.

"Here." Derrick thrust a coat at her.

She shrugged into it, thankful for the warmth. "Where are we going?"

"The lake."

He ran through the tunnels until they reached the stairs going down. In near darkness they descended, Derrick's torch adding more light for their descent. When they reached the dock, Derrick flashed the light. More eyes than she could count glittered.

"What the?" She stared at her friend.

"The leaders have decreed all the predator animals are to be killed."

Horror filled her. The cat she'd traveled with had been company and never a threat. "When?"

"In the morning." Kat started to move forward. Derrick stopped her. "I think they know they're in danger."

"So they came here." She couldn't imagine a worse place to be. Other than the stairs, there was no escape. They'd drown in the water.

A canine moved forward and growled at them.

"We're no danger to you," Kat heard herself say. "I know you don't understand me." How did one communicate with another species she knew was intelligent, yet didn't speak the same language?

She extended her hand slowly, hoping the creature didn't take her action as a hostile act.

The wolf, and somehow Kat knew it was, bared its teeth and growled again.

One of the cats moved around the wolf and sniffed Kat's fingers.

"Rerow."

The wolf stopped growling. Still, it watched her warily.

"What was that?" Derrick glanced from the animals to her.

"Not sure. A form of communication I would guess." Her eyes met his. "Just what did you have in mind?"

He rubbed the back of his neck. "Last time I checked the snow cats were being guarded. We won't be able to get near them."

Her gaze shifted to the animals standing on the dock. "Want to help?"

The gray cat moved forward. Somehow, Kat knew what they were doing. "Come on."

"What's going on?" Derrick backed away, never taking his eyes off the group.

"Derrick, it's okay."

"You can't know that."

"Yes, I can." Although how she knew, Kat wasn't sure.

Together with the animals following, they went back up the stairs and through the silent hallways. Kat couldn't even hear the ventilation running. Must have gotten much worse, more than the leaders would tell anyone and she wondered how many would perish.

"What about your sister?" he asked quietly.

"Lin wants to stay. She won't leave no matter how bad it gets."

"She'll die here."

Kat shrugged, feeling sorry for her sister. "Her choice." She'd tried to convince her sister to leave. Lin refused. Her sister would stay until the last plant withered and the heat vanished.

They reached the large bay where the snow cats were kept. The transportation sat near the door. To the side were several stacks of supplies.

She glanced at Derrick surprised. "You had this planned."

"Yeah. Help me load the stuff."

Quietly they loaded the supplies and she tried the controls. The doors creaked open. "Thought you said they were guarded."

He frowned. "They were."

Several cats jumped into the machine, followed by the wolves. Several large white with black spotted felines dashed out disappearing into the snow.

"You're welcome," Kat breathed. She crawled into the passenger seat and slammed the door.

"Where are we going?" Derrick turned the key and drove out.

"Only one computer got pinged in the city, close to where we were."

He grinned. "You snooped."

"Of course I did." She'd gotten into the records despite them being locked and knew exactly where every computer that had given a response had been. She opened her coat and pulled out a sheet of paper. "I think Mute is here," pointing to a spot on the map.

"Always wanted to meet a cat who could use a computer," Derrick muttered. He gave her an impish grin.

"Got a plan?"

"No." He shook his head.

"There's another computer they pinged." She looked over the rough map she'd drawn. "Here."

"I can't look."

On each side of them were sheer drop offs. Kat hadn't noticed when she'd left before.

"Then drive. We'll discuss it later." She looked into the back. Crammed into every available space was either a cat or wolf. "You all just sit back there and enjoy the ride. We have a place to take you."

WORD WARRIOR

"Dangerous," Tomura agreed. "Are you sure it will work my husband?"

"Yes." I hoped I sounded confident. Truth was, with the enemy we faced, I had no idea if any of us would survive.

"We need to prevent the striped one from reaching the library." Lara glanced at all the females, who crowded around waiting to hear the plan. Kittens either napped or played, not paying attention to them.

"Females still feeding young will not fight. If we begin to lose, take your kittens and run. Find a place to hide." I hoped they'd find a safe place.

If Algier had still been us, I could have sent him to talk to the males. I couldn't. They hated me and no doubt would rejoice at my death since all would be as it was before and challenges for females would begin again.

Mute sat on the counter and I saw him cock his head. He couldn't understand what we said. He and Sasha still communicated on the computer so he would have some idea what was going on. I had no doubt he would fight since he had stood beside me before to defend our females.

Mitzy scratched her ear with her hind paw. She added, "Jojo and Nan will let us know if danger threatens tonight." I hadn't forgotten she'd raised Jojo since he was a cub.

Starlite's eyes gazed at all gathered there. Rowena and Dermot, Lavena and her mate, all my wives, Indrani, and many others. "Not all will survive this battle."

"Indrani." I turned my attention to the snow ghost. "You and Jyotis are to guard the library door. Give the females with kittens time to escape if you can."

"Word Warrior," Rowena interrupted. "I can fight."

"You have cubs," I reminded her.

"He's right," Dermot agreed. "Your place as my mate is to keep them safe."

She growled at him.

"Iden, Cara and I can fight with the other wolves," Dermot promised.

"I don't like it."

"Nor I. They must survive."

Rowena said nothing more, so I continued. "Sasha, tell Mute if I do not survive, he is to lead."

"He won't like it." Sasha stood beside her mate. Sheba stood at his other side.

"I have no doubt he'll fight, but let him know if I urge him to leave, he must."

"How will you do that?"

"I'll nip his shoulder." The only idea I could come up with. "If I do, he is to leave and get all of you to safety."

"I'll tell him."

Once again I looked around at all who had come to mean much to me. Who would live and who would not?

CHAPTER 38

NAN AND JOJO

"What was that?" Nan lifted her head to listen. She could feel the warmth of Jojo's fur.

He sniffed and growled. "Stink."

She caught the smell too. "Oh, no."

"Go," he urged her. "Warn."

Slipping past her mate, she said, "Don't die," before running silently down the hall to where her father and the others waited. "The striped one is here," she announced to Word Warrior.

Indrani and Jyotis immediately took their places by the library door. Word Warrior with wives, Mute and Sasha hurried for the main door, Nan scampering ahead.

The other females and older kittens who could, took places along the hall, hiding in the debris, ready to attack.

At the door they all stopped, standing together, tails whipping back and forth, fur puffed, ready to fight. The wolves had hidden in the snow ready to spring out when needed. Nan had no idea how they could stay warm. Her mate assured her they could.

The silence of the night belied the tension all around her. Jojo stood so he shielded her, although she fully intended to use her claws.

A shape flew out of the dark, landing before Word Warrior. A huge paw swiped at him and he rolled, using the snow to cushion his fall. Bodies leapt at their attacker. Nan heard the crunch of bones, the yowls of pain, and the intense freezing growl of the striped one.

The wolves joined in, circling the invader, attacking with teeth and together just as they did when they downed prey. Jojo had taught her that, although he'd never joined them on a hunt.

The moon rose in the sky, full, giving light to the scene.

Jojo pushed her with his nose. "Go!" he ordered.

"No!" She puffed her fur and hissed.

Jojo grabbed her by the neck and ran down the hall. He dropped her inside the library.

"How bad is it?" Indrani stood beside Jojo. Nan could see he bled from his shoulder.

"Bad."

More yowls and hisses echoed from the hallway. Nan knew the striped one would be coming.

"The kittens! Get them out of here!" she ordered. She ran to the door.

Cara dashed out of a side room and stood before the white and black striped feline. It lifted a paw and Cara sprang. She sank her powerful jaws into the creature's shoulder even as its claws shredded her back.

The rest of pack joined in the attack and Nan watched as the wolves and other cats bit, scratched and finally forced the invader to floor. Indrani sprang grabbing the other by the throat and held on until the massive body stopped struggling and lay still. The snow ghost let go and coughed as if to clean her mouth of an awful taste.

"Is it dead?" Nan dared to take a few steps into the hallway.

"It's dead," Indrani assured everyone. Her long tongue began to clear away blood.

"Word Warrior," Mitzy called. "Come quickly!"

Alarmed, Nan ran after her father, Jojo beside her.

In the full light, she could see the carnage. Blood stained the snow and many cats lay dead. Among them, No!

Nan ran to her mother, who struggled to breathe. She rubbed against her, willing Tomura to fight a battle that could not be won. "Mother?"

"I go...to...Bast." Her eyes stared at nothing and Nan knew she was gone.

"Tomura." Word Warrior sank into the snow next to her, and gently touched her nose.

"Lara is gone as well," Indrani told him. "Starlite is injured. I will care for her."

"Lara too?" He saw his other wife's black and white body close by.

"For her it was quick." No doubt the healer wanted to make it easier on her father.

"Starlite?" He shuddered, getting to his feet. "Take me to her."

Near the door lay Starlite, her fur glittering as did the stars overhead. Nan licked the other's muzzle. "Stay with us."

"If I can," she promised.

Indrani took over her care and Nan moved to stand beside her father.

"Too many died." Her father would mourn. They all would.

"Mother and Lara have gone to Bast." Granted she believed in the Provider, yet she'd always honored their beliefs. "We should put their bodies with Callie."

Word Warrior said nothing.

Through the air a soft sound traveled. Nan felt it as it danced across the ground and continued.

"What was that?" She looked at her father.

He sank into the snow, saying nothing.

ALGIER

He felt his sister's hurt and lifted his head. He'd taken refuge in a crumpled house, far from anything. The endlessness of his snow-covered journey and biting cold had made him tired. If Starlite died, he did not know if he would have the strength to continue.

Maybe it would be better to die now, in the cold, far from the annoying thoughts of others.

Yet, he could not. He felt the pull and would continue until he found whatever awaited him.

POSTSCRIPT

MOON

A sound echoed through her. Moon opened her eyes knowing only the most dire of circumstances would trigger the bell. Rising, she hurried to the elevator and sat waiting. When it came, she would ride it to the surface to find her kitlings.

Hopefully, they both would survive.

ABOUT THE AUTHOR

Her cat overlords, Taj and Esther, rule her home and are very jealous of her computer when Dana Bell sits down to write. Walking on her desk and trying to sit on her keyboard are not uncommon occurrences. Still, she manages to write her many tales in a somewhat timely fashion and has completed a total of six books, along with an unknown number of short stories and some poetry which has won awards.

Her favorite hobbies are building and decorating doll houses, each with their own people who own cats, dogs and a mix of other pets. She recently discovered the joy of arranging silk flowers. Unfortunately, real ones cause her to sneeze. Among her large cat and dragon collection, is a mixture of dolls, cars, and action figures.

Happy with her current life, Dana lives in a quiet neighborhood in Colorado. Like many authors she has a day job. One must after all have a warm place for her feline companions and they like their food served promptly at breakfast, snack and dinner time. A service she happily provides.

OTHER WOLFSINGER PUBLICATIONS BOOKS BY DANA BELL

Winter Awakening –

Terrified shrieks reached Word Warrior's ears as he floundered up the embankment. In the gully below he saw the blood-stained snow and the dead corpse of the screaming kitten's mother. A stinky shaggy two-leg was trying to capture the youngster and he knew it couldn't be allowed to. With a battle cry born of his ancestors he charged down the hill—unaware of the high hunter lurking in the pines.

In the storm filled mountains, Anumati heard scratching at the entrance of her den. Her every instinct was to protect the three young who lay at her side. Her body tensed for battle as two howlers padded in.

World Warrior and Anumati are unaware kittens, pups and rightful prey are being stolen by a strange metal monster. All that is left behind are odd, jagged paw prints of an animal they do not know.

In their world of snow and biting wind they must decide if they trust each other enough to find out the truth or if old predator-prey rules remain with no hope for change.

God's Gift –

"God told us you were coming, tell us about His son."

Major Larry Henry had never expected to hear those words spoken by an alien race. Let alone one with sharp claws and fangs they used for hunting and could easily shred him, his youngest sister and her boyfriend to shreds! But when his other sister Susanna and their good friend Kal Devon disappeared from their colony, Larry and the rescue party made the astonishing discovery they weren't alone on Galilahi.

Bast's Chosen Ones & Other Cat Adventures –

Long ago in the land of the flooding Nile and sweeping sands, Bast created warriors called the Chosen Ones. They are her warriors. To them has been given the responsibility of protecting cats, whether on Earth or other worlds. Not always an easy task since often an ancient evil lurks, ready to pounce.

Not all felines walk in the goddess's domain. Some live in the far reaches of space, battling beside their humans or walk in lands long thought legend. Others tell their own version of human stories, walk as envoys of the creator, or appear as ghosts.

These cats walk where others dare not and do not prefer the comfort of cuddly lap warmers. Rather, they wish adventure, in present day, the past, or the far future.

Blood Bride (writing as Belle Blukat) –

Dr. Bertram Hoel had ignored all women he'd met until being introduced to Cira Landon at his first Science Fiction convention. Knowing he should ignore the attraction, he still takes the dangerous step to begin a relationship, aware that by doing so he is placing her life in peril.

Cira Landon wrote tales of vampire lovers unaware the handsome scientist she'd just met actually was one. Drawn to him, she finds her life threatened by an old enemy who would do anything to exact his revenge, including kidnapping her and selling her on the black market for rare blood types.

With no other options, Dr. Hoel is forced to appeal to the Elders for assistance, hoping rescue does not come too late for Cira and knowing if she is found, there is but one ancient tradition that may save her life.

CHECK OUT THESE BOOKS FROM WOLFSINGER PUBLICATIONS

The Steel Fist – Rob Jackson

The survivors of Recon 9 are needed in the Ozarks where some home-grown autocrats have taken over parts of Arkansas and parts of Missouri. They've looted National Guard armories and hoarded weapons, ammunition, and vital supplies, just waiting for the opportunity to take over the area. While most of their transport, armor, and aircraft are obsolete, they face people with no protection against such deadly equipment. And they're trying to get the local natural resources to gain control of weapons that even the military have no defense against.

Recon 9 has gained four new members and formed an alliance with locals, many of them veterans, against a common enemy. The locals have some grasp of tactics, an excellent knowledge of the hilly, forested countryside and a burning desire to be rid of the terrorists, who call themselves:

THE STEEL FIST

Crisis in Big-G City – S.D. Matley

Olympus, Inc., is locked in battle with climate change!

Athena's Secret Ops program steps in when bad boy and technological genius Hermes can't come up with a carbon-curbing solution. Undercover agents Cleo Petra and Pan are deployed in the mortal world to vanquish the notorious East brothers, chthonic fossil fuel magnates who pass as human and eat humans, too...

Two-month-old Pablo, the one-quarter chthonic infant son of two fathers formerly known as P.B., employs his extraordinary abilities of adult speech and intellect in pursuit of climate justice!

Meanwhile, David Bernstein, whose hot romance with Cleo Petra meets a rocky end, recovers the memory of his century-old love affair with a beautiful Spanish nurse. He time travels to 1918 to find her and encounters love, loss, and the City of Mount Olympus —a dark and sinister place where every inhabitant lives in fear of volatile and destructive Zeus!

David's birth father and Hera's former fling, Saul Crispin, is outed as a mortal made immortal. Will Hera's high crime of granting Saul eternal life land her before a jury of her peers for judgment?

And what of baby-crazy Queen of the Underworld, Persephone, pregnant at last but not by Hades?

Intrigue, espionage, crimes of passion, secret babies and looming existential threats—everywhere you look there's a Crisis in Big-G City!

Tree of Bones – Book Two: A Familiar's Tale
- Verna McKinnon

Two Curses

A curse of Darkness... Deep within the Thill forest, stands a tree made of human bones, crowned in black leaves and red thorns.

A curse of Light... Beneath the Wastelands of Skarros, a crystal imprisons a dark, immortal queen.

The Sorceress, Runa, is tormented by horrific images of this tree of bones in a distant, lifeless forest. Even as the visions debilitate her, Mellypip, her beloved familiar, also experiences these sinister dreams, bound by the same dream seer magic as his mistress. The tree of bones summons Runa, and she must risk madness and death as obsession drives her on. What she finds reveals a devastating truth.

Koll the Sorcerer awaits trial for his crimes. His familiar, Xabral, searches for allies to free him. Driven by his own dreams of dark prophecy, Koll seeks to free Obsydia, the Bloodstone Queen, from her prison. Determined to let nothing stop him, Koll will commit any evil to achieve his goal.

Runa and Mellypip's newest journey reveals truths behind ancient secrets, as Koll's obsessive hunt for a fallen queen threatens to doom the world forever. Runa and Koll, bound by opposing magical destinies of Light and Dark, will ultimately face frightening revelations and unimagined consequences.

Gate of Souls – Book One: A Familiar's Tale
- Verna McKinnon

Familiars.
Magical animal companions of sorcerers.

Keepers of spells and secrets.

Most important, devoted friends for life.

When one such familiar, Mellypip, bonds with the young sorceress Runa, he shares in the wonders of magic. Together, Mellypip and Runa train under the tutelage of Runa's grandfather, Cathal, and his cantankerous mountain owl familiar, Belwyn. But secrets and spells do not make for good sorcery. Old friends begin to vanish even as enemies from Cathal's past return, threatening to reveal the truth of Runa's parents; a truth from which Cathal must protect his granddaughter at any cost. When Cathal is kidnapped, Runa and Mellypip rush against time to save their family and friends from dark sorcery that will not only destroy them, but shatter the Gate of Souls and release demonic creatures of The Otherworld into the mortal realms.

The Seven Exalted Orders – Deby Fredericks

Arkanost has Seven Exalted Orders. No more, no less. When a magus goes renegade in a far-off province, the Mage Lords demand something be done.

Ryamon is bitter and frustrated. He longs to be a Fire magus; as a Stone magus, he's miserable. If he can bring the rogue back, he has a chance—his last chance—to fulfill his dream.

It's a great plan—until he actually meets Valdira.

Tails from the Front Lines 2: The Thin Blue Line – edited by Carol Hightshoe

Come meet some of the four-legged members of Law Enforcement who also serve and protect.

Here our authors will introduce you to the brave K9 officers who serve alongside their human partners. They are their eyes, ears, noses and sometimes when necessary they are their shield, protecting others.

Proceeds from this anthology will be donated to the El Paso County (Colorado) Sheriff's Office K9 program in memory of K9 Jinx who was killed in the line of duty on April 11, 2022.

Ring of Fire – edited by Dana Bell

Enter the Ring of Fire, as unpredictable as the land masses shaking a city and volcanoes erupting covering the landscape. Could there be other reasons for these events? Or could these rings be more than a geological location.

They may be dragons playing tricks
or magic portals opened to mysterious realms
or sacrificing the best work of a lifetime.
Perhaps a rescue during a forest fire
or an attempt to raise the dead
or even while attending a high school reunion.

Journeys are taken to far off lands, another world, and through caves, each with their own unique twist.

Each tale presents a new idea on what the Ring of Fire could be. It is more than what many have been led to believe. Pull up a chair and warm yourself by our fires—just don't let yourself get burned.

Coyote – Charles Combee

While camping in a remote canyon in Utah Jim accidently sees an ancient rite taking place with a coyote like creature presiding over it. Now this creature wants Jim dead.

Audrey and her family go hiking in Utah and are attacked by this creature. Audrey is the only survivor, but she is pulled into a strange world of darkness and glass. She is 'rescued' by Jim, but is still linked to the creature, whose hold on her will end in her death unless Jim can find a way to break that link.

In his dreams, or are they ancient memories, Jim begins to learn more about Coyote as well as the magics that previously bound him. But those dreams end without teaching him the full magics. Can he find a way to free Audrey and stop Coyote from once again terrorizing humankind?

Believing is Seeing – Joanna Michal Hoyt

What we believe shapes what we see. Sometimes the stories we tell free us. Sometimes they trap us.

Some people see things their neighbors can't or won't see. Are they inspired? Delusional? Who decides?

As the faithful people of her village cry out for their god's help in disaster, a young peasant woman faces the terrifying possibility that she may be that god.

A time-traveling Jewish refugee visits 21st-century churches and confronts almost unrecognizable versions of himself.

Three troubled people make the dangerous visit to The Library where the maddening stories lodged inside them can be removed—on certain demanding conditions.

Having been warned away from the vacant lot which is said to house a portal to Hell, the new girl in town naturally goes to investigate.

Early in the grid collapse—or apocalypse?—a Christian lesbian farm couple paint "WELCOME" on their barn and await visitors.

An old man in the Terran diaspora enlists in a crusade to save humanity and belatedly wonders if he's on the wrong side.

Step inside these stories and see what you believe—but don't believe everything you see.

Out of the Darkness – edited by Carol Hightshoe

Mental Health issues have long been stigmatized, with those facing them pushed into the shadows, often unable to deal with the darkness they find themselves trapped in.

In this collection, stories explore many types of darkness—Suicidal Ideation, Death from Suicide, Survivor's Guilt, PTSD, Chronic Pain, Chronic Illness, Depression, Death of a Loved One, Secrets, Bullying, and other forms of darkness are explored. Some related to mental health issues and some not, but all of them offer very human perspectives. As in real life, some stories have happy endings and sadly others don't.

We offer these stories of darkness without judgement, but with hope and compassion. Some roads should never have to be traveled—but we understand that for many they are being traveled alone.

Proceeds from sales of Out of the Darkness will be donated to the American Foundation for Suicide Prevention—or more information on AFSP please visit their website at: afsp.org.

Never Cheat a Witch – edited by Carol Hightshoe

Magical curses. Arcane revenge. Being transformed into a frog. Things evil witches do to mere mortals who cross their path. But, what if there is more to the story...

Deals made with a witch are magically binding and can bring dire consequences to those who even think about breaking them.

Whether they are seeking revenge for wrongs done to them, helping others or simply trying to live their lives—it is NEVER wise to try and cheat a witch.

Open your spell book and join our authors as they relate tales of witches and mortals. From classic fantasy witches to modern day witches and even the legendary Baba Yaga. Good and Evil as well as every shade of gray in between.

And, yes—there is a prince who is turned into a frog.

Return of the Black Witch – M.R. Williamson

One should not expect to slap the hand of an old crone and expect to walk away without at least a limp. The old witch Ethrel Ibenus is up to her tricks again and this time they've turned deadly. But where did her spirit go after Professor Martin shot her with his wee pistol?

Now, all are looking for the crone's familiar, Seleene. But the big timber wolf cannot be found. The search for the spirit of Ibenus now begins in earnest. Will Entwhistle and her Dwarves be able to help? Perhaps the Green Witch Pereen will be able to use a crystal derived from one of the Witch's own spells will do the trick. Fearing failure, Entwhistle improvises a plan 'C', the use of a mythical creature once thought to be long dead.

Time Capsules – edited by Carol Hightshoe

Time Capsules—history and mystery—a gift or a message from the past to the future.

Messages that can easily be misunderstood.

What were the reasons for passing along a pair of pink, fuzzy handcuffs?

A glass vial containing a perfect dandelion puff?

A Japanese Katana?

A red and blue scarf?

A wooden spoon?

What magic do these items contain? What stories do they tell?

From the past to the future. Mysteries and meanings abound within these pages, as well as reminders of the things people find precious. What will you find?

US/THEM – edited by Carol Hightshoe

US/THEM – THEM/US

Fear of the Other breeds hatred of the Other

They aren't like us—so they must be bad…inferior… dangerous…

Humans are by nature social animals, but we tend to bond with other humans with whom we have something in common: beliefs, experiences, likes and dislikes, etc.

With the expansion of humans across the planet, it seems that, even as our numbers grow, we find ways to whittle our groups into ever narrower, specialized, and exclusive blocks. We target the Other for the most minor differences and interpret everything from THEM as an insult or an attack.

Within these pages you will witness hatred, intolerance and fanaticism as well as love, understanding and acceptance. Most of all, I, and the authors, hope you discover stories that will cause you to pause and think before condemning someone as being THEM and not US.

And more – check out our books at
www.wolfsingerpubs.com

www.ingramcontent.com/pod-product-compliance
Lightning Source LLC
Chambersburg PA
CBHW070750180626
46818CB00007B/3056